I, ROBERT'S ROBOT AND OTHER STORIES

Marvel Chukwudi Pephel

Mwanaka Media and Publishing Pvt Ltd,
Chitungwiza Zimbabwe
*
Creativity, Wisdom and Beauty

Publisher: *Mmap*
Mwanaka Media and Publishing Pvt Ltd
24 Svosve Road, Zengeza 1
Chitungwiza Zimbabwe
mwanaka@yahoo.com
mwanaka13@gmail.com
www.africanbookscollective.com/publishers/mwanaka-media-and-publishing
https://facebook.com/MwanakaMediaAndPublishing/

Distributed in and outside N. America by African Books Collective
orders@africanbookscollective.com
www.africanbookscollective.com

ISBN: 978-1-77934-079-5
EAN: 9781779340795

DISCLAIMER
All views expressed in this publication are those of the author and do
not necessarily reflect the views of *Mmap*.

ACKNOWLEDGEMENT

My deepest gratitude goes to everyone, especially friends who read my initial stories. Again to online magazines where all the stories, except The Orchestra of Frogs, has been published. Again to Sevhage Publishers who shortlisted The Boy Who Fell From The Sky in their 2019 Short Story Prize. It feels surreal right now that all my wild dreams has found expression in book form. I have always hoped that my books would be what readers would rather have tucked beneath their pillows than on a bookshelf. I do hope this begins to do that. And I do believe readers may begin to see how great the breadth of their imagination can be, and how stories can unite us. And to quote Ralph Waldo Emerson, I must say: "If we must meet, then we have through these pages met".

DEDICATION

To all those who walked that I may run.

TABLE OF CONTENTS

CHAPTER ONE:

PRINCESS ALWAYS

When we left Nigeria that morning, we did not know we left behind a part of us. We did not know we would soon be evaluating things. Kate had died leaving her alter ego with the risk of sinking into oblivion. One thing with voicing a cartoon character is that the voice-giver ought to be available for as long as the series would run. Most times, nobody puts in proactive measures with regards to the absence of the "voice". So when Kate died from an undisclosed circumstance, Blue Moon Studios went into sheer disarray. The character *Princess Always,* the children's favourite, needed a quick voice replacement if the series must continue to run. The cartoon *Find Me a Prince* was already a commercial success, having sold millions of copies within few months of its release -- who would expect Blue Moon Studios to let go of its profitable venture? In a mad bid to find a voice replacement, a subtle advert was placed on the internet. I was the one who saw the advert, and by the next day I had informed Ifeoma, Chioma, and Oge about it. All three of them were excited by the prospect of travelling to Hollywood if anyone of them was selected as the winner of the contract. I was excited too -- at least I could bask in the reflected glory. We read the rules carefully and subsequently sought for help online, since we've never voiced a cartoon character before. Google was kind, as usual, with its directions. We learned that we needed to take a professional voice-over class, and so we searched for an online studio offering reputable online classes at a cheap rate. We found one we thought was better and enrolled. We did everything we were told -- I ensured none of the girls were lazy on this. I even practised with them. We were advised to try different cartoon voices as versatility gives one a better edge, and leaves him standing in good stead. We complied. Blue Moon Studios' *Find Me a Prince* was their cash cow, and we were eager to land the contract which translated to millions of naira. When we felt sufficiently confident enough, we proceeded to record a demo of our cartoon voices. The rules stipulated that the demo duration be 30- to 60-second demo, and we heeded. Before we did the final thing which was submitting, we prayed. The girls took the prayer serious, and I saw the glaring reason -- contract worth millions of naira to be won! After the prayer, the girls clustered around me while I operated my laptop.

It is amazing how people can believe in the possibility of their success, even when they are in competition with the world. It is just that amazing!

We read the rules once more before we submitted our mp3s to the email address provided. When we were done submitting, we hugged each other and hoped for the best.

***

The next day, I rode pillion on a commercial motorcycle known as *okada* to the outskirts of town. My foods and beverages were almost finished, and so I went to market. Ekere Market was not the nearest market, but it was the cheapest -- not even transport fare could erase its cheapness. I reached the market with my clothes wet -- it was drizzling when I left my lodge. I paid the okada man and ran across the road, ducking and slipping past the pile of planks a man was carrying on his head. I considered myself lucky. I could hear the man shouting curses at me as I run into a shop. The shop belonged to a woman heavily inclined to *embonpoint* -- a woman so fat you could barely notice a neck. She was jovial and came across to me as a woman who loves youths. I haggled prices for a few things, and would have purchased everything I needed from her shop had she not run out of stock for some of the things on my list. I bought the remaining things elsewhere and returned to my lodge at exactly 2.14 pm. I usually took note of departure and arrival times!

***

I was in my room on the 16th of August, 2001, playing Tupac's songs aloud with my home theater when Chioma phoned me. She said she was coming to see me urgently, and I told her I was around and would be waiting, would be expectant. It was already two months, and I had not remembered the Blue Moon Studios Competition. I still did not remember until she arrived my lodge. Chioma was in the same department with me at the university, but not the same level. I was above her by a gap of two years. I was lying on the futon my uncle based in Canada had gifted me, when a knock came. I rose immediately and went for the door.

"Jideofor!" Chioma shouted as soon as I opened the door. "Jideofor, celebration is in the air!"
    "What?" I asked in a daze.
    "Provide the glasses," she said, producing a bottle of wine from the nylon she was carrying.

"What for? Did you ace an exam? Did you win something?" I asked before I suddenly remembered. "Blue Moon Studios?"

"Yes, boy, we won!"

"We won? Yes!" I grabbed her in excitement, so hard she was begging to be released. "Yes, I will get the glasses. Did you inform Oge and Ifeoma?"

"Yes, they are having tutorials. They will join us later."

That day, we celebrated until we were filled, wasted and sleepy.

***

Tinseltown kept calling and tugging at our minds. As an exclusive privilege, "the winner of the contract could come along with someone on an all-expense-paid trip". The two of us would be going -- I and Chioma. She was very much excited and thankful to me. Prior to September 9 when we had to heed the call of Tinseltown, we went shopping with our money. I burnt my Tupac CDs into my laptop. We visited the American Embassy and ensured our visas and other requirements were ready. We agreed not to tell our parents, and we stuck to our plans. Good for us, we were on vacation! Living at Lagos meant we didn't travel back at the end of every semester- a problem of expenses. Gladly, we waited and waited. When September 9 finally came, we were over-ready. Over-prepared.

Straight to Murtala Mohammed International Airport we went. That morning, a Saturday morning, we felt quite different from our usual selves. Who would not, when his or her life is or about becoming interesting? We arrived early enough to be able to engage in discussions and the observation of the facial expressions of people. We wondered if it was possible to tell a first-timer by their facial expression. We wondered if our facial expression or composure had given us out as first-time travellers. Through the final waiting minutes, we sat still and watched.

Soon our departure time came, and we went aboard the plane. Oh, did I tell you about the long waiting hours at the security line? It was gruesome, and you would probably not want to hear it. I was told, later, that airports have to do their jobs to ensure drugs, bombs or illegal items do not get onto the departing airplane. Not like I didn't watch movies.

We zipped through the sky to our destination.

While in flight, I wore my headphones and listened to my rap songs. Chioma took out her book, *When You Fall In Love, Break A Leg*, and read seriously. I wondered if anyone on the plane knew we were going to Hollywood, that we were VIPs. From song-playing I transitioned to sleeping, and only woke up when the stewardess announced our arrival in America. I turned and caught Chioma's eyes in time to give her a look of importance. We smiled.

***

We took a taxi immediately we stepped down the plane, and called to inform them we had just arrived in America. The taxi driver was a blonde, and that was my first time of seeing a blonde person in real life. There was an obvious briskness in his attitude.

"You two really must be coming from Africa, I guess." He said this casually.

We remained silent.

"Hello," he said trying to catch a glimpse of our faces through the mirror above his head, "Where are you guys from?"

"Africa," Chioma replied, almost rudely.

"Of course! Which country?"

"Nigeria." I replied, quite contemplating.

"Oh, Nigeria! The most populous black nation! Have you got any animal skins?"

Silence.

"Hello, do you have any animal skin with you?"

"Please, drive us to our destination!" I was the one who spoke, and my voice felt shaky- it could have been anger or sheer disgust. It irked me that someone could only relate to my human-ness in the light of animal skins. It irked me that one would think Africa is more populated by animals than humans. If we had argued, his argument would have been tangential- he would have avoided making his point obvious. The rest of the ride was without discussions, and I loved it. When we reached our destination, the blonde guy told us to be quick with our luggage. We alighted and paid him his money.

The next drive took us to the designated hotel. We were warmly welcomed, although a particular concierge gave us cold shoulders. It had never occurred to me that I was extremely black- so black a *coloured* American would appear to be white when standing next to me. I had only learned about racial relations in newspapers and school texts. Chioma, too, was this black. With the few reactions we had received so far, we began to evaluate things. We started to wonder what the reaction of the people expecting us would be. Maybe it would be strictly business, we thought. After all, we had what they wanted. Our hotel room was an expensive one- ebony tables, amazing portraits, a large television set, and many more. We were comfortable. Within few hours of our settling down, our attention focused on a particular painting on the wall. It was a silhouette of a man pointing a gun to his head, while a woman knelt by his leg and polishing his big shoe. There was something about the painting that haunted me for long. My mind had a picture of what it portrayed, but words did always fail me. We spent the rest of the day eating, drinking and chatting.

***

We waited to be picked up for the job on September 11, 2001. That morning, I had called my mom to hear her voice- something I wasn't fond of doing. I equally felt an odd sensation in my right ear, and was helping myself out with a cotton bud when our car arrived. I picked my briefcase and laptop, and we walked towards the car where the driver, a tall serious-looking man on black suit, was waiting. The car looked more functional than classy or sexy. He opened the back door for us and we went in. At the back of the car, with us, was a man in police uniform. He kept staring at his wrist where a watch was fastened and staring out the window as the car navigated through streets and thoroughfares. On occasions, he would make a call which always reassured the receiver that he was coming with us. We were relaxed and unsuspecting. We just couldn't wait to meet the folks at Blue Moon Studios. Never did we know that our reaching Blue Moon Studios would be stalled. The car had just parked in front of the police station, when the policeman who rode with us brought out his handcuffs and asked us to step out. We were scared and confused at once.

"Sir, what have we done?" I asked, twisting my accent to sound like an American.

He gave us a scowl and began to take us along with him. This place is not Blue Moon Studios, I had thought. And so, the thought of going into a police station instead of a studio, an animation studio, left me burning and seething with frustration. Before we were detained, a high-ranking police officer with a wide moustache asked us, especially me:

"You both are terrorists, aren't you?"

"No, sir!" we answered in unison.

His eyes still fixed on me: "Boy, you'd better co-operate to avoid torture. You just flew into America a couple of days and the World Trade Centre is burning. How do you explain that?"

"The World Trade Centre?" I asked in sheer ignorance.

"Yes, the World Trade Centre. Who are the masterminds?"

"Sir, I know nothing about this. I swear!" Tears were beginning to form in my eyes. I couldn't imagine coming to America for the sake of a cartoon character and ending up in jail for something as serious as terrorism. Chioma was already sobbing.

"Sir, please, we know nothing about the burning World Trade Centre. We are in America to voice a cartoon character." Chioma cried.

The moustached police officer turned towards Chioma with surprise on his face, and then burst into laughter.

"Ha ha, ho ho," he chortled. "Cartoon? Officers, please take them into protective custody."

"Yes, sir!" the officers answered, and took us away.

***

While in a different cell, with no contact with Chioma, I began to think about the incident that brought us into where we found ourselves. Why would someone decide to destroy somewhere as busy and important as the World Trade Centre? What did he stand to gain? The newspaper which a prison guard had just given me lay beside me. I was not in the right frame of mind nor had the interest to flip through its pages. But when I could not think anymore, I grabbed it from the ground and perused through it. It was the morning of the next day. There were speculations pointing towards an Islamic mastermind; particularly, Osama bin Laden. I read a little and lost the interest to continue. This was not why I came to America, I thought. I remembered the World Conference against Racism (WCAR) which was held at the Durban International Convention Centre in Durban, South Africa from 31 August to 8 September, 2001 and knew this World Trade Centre attack would overshadow its essence and any change it could have brought. I wondered, right there in the soul-sapping cell, if Blue Moon Studios have a hand in our arrest. And if they did not, I wondered if they were looking for us. My mind became a room of worries. Perhaps the cold-shoulder-giving concierge had a hand in our fate. Towards the evening, as Heavens might have it, a guard came to inform me that some executives from Blue Moon Studios had come to see me. What took them so long?!

***

The next day, a black limousine came to pick us. A neatly dressed man opened the door for us, and we fell in. He was smiling, but it looked more practised than natural. Once we were in, he stepped in and the driver zoomed off.

"Princess Always?" the neatly dressed man sitting opposite us asked, like there was another Princess something he was also expecting.

"Yes," I answered. And that was the only discussion until we reached the entrance to Hollywood. Somehow, I did not see the famous "Hollywood" sign in the mountains -- maybe my eyes missed it or it was not visible from such ground level. It's in the mountains, of course!

Beautiful landscape, beautiful scenery, beautiful buildings. A world of its own! The neatly dressed man opened the door with the same old smile, and we stepped out with a gasp. Chioma held my hand as we stared with broad smiles. The same man brought us back to reality with the order to follow him. We obeyed. Any white face we passed stared at us for long. We were new and different, and we knew it! At a magnificent door, we stood and watched the man press a button which flung the door open. We walked through it and went immediately to a moving flight of stairs. We stepped down to the other side of the building. We passed the bust of a legendary Hollywood actor, whose nose I felt with my fingers, before we reached a heavy glass door. The neatly dressed man, whom someone had called John, entered a password and the door opened. Two ladies approached us as soon as we entered.

"John," one of them began, "Princess Always?"

"Yes," John replied calmly. "Real Africans." His reply made it sound like they had expected a white person to win the contract, or at least expected a Black with refined and polished skin.

The other woman observed us calmly and carefully.

"Come right away!" the same one who spoke to John said. "Mr Brown is waiting." Her hips were swinging from side to side in fast movements, and I feared she might fall from her sleek stiletto. We passed two doors before we entered the studio- a large, fine sound-proof area. A tall pot-bellied man was sitting on a swivel chair, turning here and there. He stood up when he saw us.

"Princess Always, I guess." His voice was theatrical.

"Yes, sir!" replied the ever-talking woman.

"Good. Now we can have *Find Me a Prince* up and running. Hey, John, come give me a hand!" John moved quickly towards him while the calm lady offered us seats. When Mr Brown and John were done setting up equipment, they returned to us.

"Yeah, you don't know how happy I am. Like you read online, Kate died from a circumstance undisclosed to us. Her people chose to keep everything secret and private. Well, enough of the tragedy! What's your name?" He pointed at Chioma.

"Chioma."

He hesitated before he opened his mouth: "Chai-o-ma! Good, good." Without knowing that he had murdered the name, he turned to me. "And you?"

"Jideofor."

"Okay, auteur, come please!" He was referring to a Zimbabwean-American whose name was Panashe, or maybe Tinashe, who was so soft-spoken and graceful I began to envy such exquisite nature. After a little discussion, he pointed at Chioma.

"Come and wear this head device."

I stepped forward, instead of Chioma.

Before I forget, sorry I didn't tell you it was my voice that matched the Kate-Princess Always voice. None of the girls' demo was appropriate or suitable, and I took Chioma along because she was my best friend.

"What is wrong with you?" Mr Brown asked, his eyes filled with contempt. "Are you Chioma?"

"No, sir! I am...I am Princess Always."

"You are who?" he asked *sans* patience.

"I meant...my name is Jideofor, but I am Princess Always. I will be voicing..."

"You will be doing what?"

"Yes sir, Princess Always!"

Mr Brown burned with rage. I do not blame him; who would expect a man to be able to twist his voice so well to match a seemingly rare feminine voice?

"Are you an impostor?" he asked, clenching his fist.

"No, no. I am not, sir!" Tears were already forming in my eyes; an involuntary action that made me feel ashamed. Perhaps, America is not for me, I thought. He approached me and buried his fist in my stomach.

When I regained consciousness, I was on a hospital bed.

***

When I woke up, the thought of my mom clawed at my mind. Poor woman, she would think her son is at the university reading books or making notes- lo! I am going through a series of troubles in America. I shook my head and wiped the tear-drop on my cheek. There were bruises on my forehead, because Mr Brown kicked me on the head before I blacked out. I do not blame him. I was looking at the ceiling thoughtlessly, when Chioma walked in through the door. She looked weary and cold. In her hand was a note, which she gave me afterwards and began to touch me with pity in her eyes. I took the note. It had the name of Mr Brown on it. He had written to tell me about his battle, how he has anger management issues. He said so many things, but only one sentence ricocheted on my mind-walls and settled incomprehensible (or was it unacceptable?):

"Jideofor, I apologise for hurting you; I blame it on my madness, and you can be Princess Always as much as you'd want."

I sighed after reading it, and my pains seemed to increase by a hundred-fold. I would be discharged in two days' time, and I could not wait to return to Nigeria. I could not wait to return to myself.

Today, when I look back to those experiences, I just laugh and laugh and laugh.

CHAPTER TWO

THE INDEPENDENT   JAN. 01, 2901.
Serving you the fresh and honest!

NORA'S COLUMN
Edited by Nora Agbajambee.
               Story title: **I, ROBERT'S ROBOT**
Warri, 2900.
   A tiger does not lose sleep over the opinion of sheep - not when a sheep is a sheep.
       - Robert Maduka (Ph.D).

1a.
The notice made public by Mr. and Mrs. Dike read: "A babysitter needed at 25 Queens Close. Must be a young female. Preferred age bracket: 20-29. Must know how to speak French. Must know how to take care of a baby, how to wash all things washable. Must know how to make judicious use of time. Must be decent. Must be eager to work at any given time and circumstance. Interested persons must apply in person and should call this phone number, 0700 255 5888. Thank you." Mr. and Mrs. Dike had not been married for long - just eighteen months. The baby to be babysitted was their first issue. The couple had busy lives - husband a pilot, wife a banker. So it was quite reasonable for them to want the services of a babysitter. The notice was publicized in newspapers in Senegal and Nigeria. Wife's Senegalese, husband's Nigerian. Getting a

babysitter was the wife's idea, which explains the French language preference. If you thought as much, you have a nimble mind: *A babysitter all the way from Senegal?* Never worry. Mrs. Dike could afford to foot the expenses involved in "importing" a Senegalese babysitter as long as she satisfies her desired qualifications. In fact, she could even direct such persons to her sister's house in Senegal where her sister could do the first assessment. And so that was how they got Suzzy, a Senegalese girl in her early twenties. Suzzy was a very beautiful and nice-looking lady. She had an accent that sounded sexy - but this was not why she was employed. She was meant to be taking care of baby and not sounding sexy. So Mrs. Dike, fearing her husband may fall for this sexy accent of a thing, asked her to try and shove the sexy accent down her throat if she could. But no, she couldn't. It was no acting - it was a natural thing. And Mrs. Dike felt lucky that her husband was the busy type. Suzzy appeared to be a very respectful and obedient girl, and so Mrs. Dike had not much to worry about. And Mrs. Dike believed Baby Sandra was in good hands. Mr. Dike after engaging the young woman in a lengthy discussion discovered she was very intelligent and promised to take her along whenever there was a conference or symposium he needed to attend. When he made the promise, Suzzy smiled and genuflected while thanking him. *Merci Monsieur!*

1b.

And it so happened that on one occasion Mr. Dike drove the babysitter and the baby to a symposium. He was fulfilling his promise. The symposium was on the subject of Modern Technology. At the end of the symposium, Mr. Dike introduced Suzzy to Dr. Robert Maduka, a Cybernetic Engineer and Mr. Fitzpatrick Baumbach, a Cyborg Anthropologist. Amongst the two men, it was Dr. Robert who still had the single marital status. And to the excitement of Mr. Dike, Dr. Robert quickly showed an interest in the young woman. He left them to talk and went to wait in his car.

2a.

I am Robert's robot. Because I am my master's creation, you can call me Robert the robot. I was assembled on a Wednesday. In the process of assembling me, master made a mistake. And that mistake in creation is the flaw that I now have. I can remember how it all started. Listen, let me tell you:

It was a cool weather Wednesday. Robert's face took a swift change as his tongue felt the tang of the lemon he had plucked from the university's orchard. As he always did, he ate in tandem with pressing his phone - a habit he would not drop in a hurry. He was a young man who looked like he was, wait for it, 35! Gene, gene, gene, he would often defensively say. He was big. Thankfully, he played basketball for The Movers - and his teammates and others often called him Shaker O'Neal after Shaquille O'Neal. Robert, or Shaker O'Neal, was a player whose swift turns were ferocious and brutal - head-hittings and jaw-jabbings were often the case. He was a final year student of Cybernetics. He had started work on me during his sophomore days, this I know from reading a personal journal he kept. However, it was during the time he was writing his thesis that he finished my creation. It was a cool weather Wednesday, but he was sweating profusely when my consciousness became fully-formed. The lemon dropped from his hand. When I jerked my leg in a forward motion, a smile of triumph sprouted upon his face. The thing with existing in-between two worlds is that you have the opportunity to know almost enough about both worlds. So before I became fully created, I already knew many things about humans and the Earth. Believe me, I came alive prepared. And so when

I moved my second leg, Robert ran around his room. He came back to me and manacled my feet. I was furious and wished I had already mastered bodily movements, because that's the only reason why I didn't land Robert a ferocious uppercut. I dreaded the idea of being a slave. Well, I am a different kind of robot. The kind that has AI that gives autonomy. In other words, I can think for myself. A uniqueness that is tremendously advantageous. But then, as I have not told you, there is a flaw deep within the core of my being that wouldn't allow me to choose one thought over the other. The choice of algorithm and the reckless ingenuity of my master are the main pillars of my flaw. This flaw allows me to carry out two thought processes at the same time. This means I get to act based on two impulses. I get to carry out a two-in-one action. It's a wonderful flaw! Imagine fighting and dancing. Imagine killing someone while also wanting to save him. Such a flaw! Flaw too deep for comfort. Listen, I am not a bad robot - neither was I created to be. Since I was born, I have been trying to keep self-destruction at bay. More so, I try my utmost best to make sure I do not hurt humans. I always try to steer away from cavalier actions.

Okay, that's the brief account of my becoming. To be honest, Robert's life has never been any better until my coming. I have made him proud on many occasions. Let me narrate to you one incident:

It is good to have neighbours, especially those like Aaron who is a ventriloquist who is extremely amiable. But not knowing the true identity of your neighbour is another thing. Aaron was one of our new neighbours. He moved in before Robert, I and his niece. He was a man in his twenties who looked like he wouldn't be able to hurt a fly. And due to his extraordinary friendliness and the ventriloquist thing, Robert began to call him Aarondy out of fondness. But

then, in his absence, Aarondy metamorphosed into a man wearing the tag "Z".
Z that must peer through his window.

Inside the house was Robert's niece, Chika, who was grounded by Robert.
Inside the house, Chika was already feeling like she was shut out of paradise.
Inside the house was I too. There was no video games to play, neither was there
a friend to call nor television to watch. She sat on the sofa and it was not good
for her. She sat on the rug and it irritated her. She ate her favourite food and it
seemed salty and rancid all at once. She drank water and it seemed to have
taste. Nothing seemed to please her. She sat by the grand piano she had brought
into the living room and tried to play something that could be soothing or
comforting. And Z, binoculars in his eyes, peered through the window. With
great interest, he peered through his neighbour's window.

Chika woke up the following day wearing only her underwears. She yawned
and went to brush her teeth. Just as she stood in front of the bathroom mirror,
toothbrush in mouth, she saw how unhappy she looked. She blamed herself for
joining the girl nicknamed Pinky to visit someone she didn't know. After all
that was how she joined the gang of drug addicts. She frowned and began to
brush her teeth. When she was done brushing, she walked with reckless
abandon to the kitchen. She collected the tureen on the kitchen counter and
poured the content of the tureen into a small pot. She switched on the gas cooker
and began to warm the content. After the food steamed for some time, she
switched off the gas cooker and walked into her bedroom to pick a hairbrush.
She returned to the living room only to see through the window what seemed
normal at first and suspicious later. I kept following her around even though she
was often saying something like, "This robot, I need some privacy."

On a ha-ha perched a vulture, a vulture, before there were three when Chika
looked again. She, while trying to wear her skirt, tried to get close to the

23

window. She buttoned up the skirt and reached the window in time to see Aarondy dragging a big sack to his van. He looked like a man in a hurry to get something done or to be done with something. Chika watched carefully, paying attention to details. Aarondy lifted the sack into his van and Chika saw how heavy the sack was for him. She watched him take off his leather gloves before entering his van. And he drove off leaving a red stain on the ground. And of course I was recording everything with my inbuilt cameras.

She had forgotten about seeing Aarondy dragging an oddly-shaped sack the day before, and the red liquid that stayed on the ground after he lifted the sack into his van. All that mattered to her now was the novel she was engrossed in. And all that mattered to Aarondy, who could also be called Z, was how to get in.
He looked around himself and rubbed the left edge of his mouth. It was cold outside and he was wearing his mittens. He considered climbing onto the ledge outside his neighbour's window, his neighbour whose niece was often home alone these days. He mistakingly kicked down a flower pot and tried to raise it. When he raised his head, binoculars in his eyes, he realised that the girl reading was now looking in his direction. He gasped and disappeared with his binoculars. Chika arrived at the closed window, waving him to come back. But Aarondy and Z didn't look like they wanted to talk. At least, not with someone they were spying on.

So, after Chika served her punishment, curiosity got a better part of me. I started comparing footages in my memory's archive. And, lo and behold, Aarondy was the notorious serial killer who often killed teenage girls. That was how I helped to solve a crime puzzle and Aarondy was arrested. My importance is undisputedly invaluable. I am not even boasting. But if I ever do, I should get an applause for it. What have I not done to keep my master safe? What have I not done to make him proud?

And how did he choose to pay me back? By getting a girlfriend that will take his attention from me! Such an unfair thing to do! Humans. Don't tell me you are different - you all are like two peas in a pod! Since master fell in love with Suzzy, he no longer gives me enough attention. It suddenly became Suzzy this, Suzzy that. And I gradually became mad and furious. Everyday, I fought for my master's attention. In fact, the one that irked me most was that this Suzzy was not as educated as Robert the human. I know you humans will ask me what I know about love. Humans. So because I am made of metal I should not demand love? Humans. H-U-M-A-N-S = Humans! And while I was still lamenting over my master's attention that was stolen by Suzzy, master made an immigrant Russian philosopher his acquaintance. Before I knew what was happening, the little attention I could have managed after Suzzy had taken the greater portion was now used by my master for philosophical musings. Since the Russian philosopher came into his life, he started keeping a personal journal he titled *Suggested Serving*. On the first page of the book was the saying he became fond of using: *A tiger does not lose sleep over the opinion of sheep - not when a sheep is a sheep.* In this same journal, he showed some interest in poetry. Believe me, there was a line that made me discover I could laugh for the first time. Imagine. I really think he writes quite fine poetry for an amateur and hobbyist like him. Even though I appreciated what he was doing with his time, that can never be an excuse to neglect me. So when it became too much for me to bear, I sought a way to get my master's attention back.

2b.

On one fateful day, I found myself using master's saying continuously. I couldn't tell why it kept ringing in my memory. *A tiger does not lose sleep over the opinion of sheep - not when a sheep is a sheep! A tiger does not lose sleep over the opinion of sheep - not when a sheep is a sheep!!* Oh, Lord! I said and went to sit on the seat specially-made for me. Each time I say, *Oh, Lord,* master seemed to have a particular expression of confusion on his face. No wonder I found "To which god do androids pray?" in his *Suggested Serving.* Back to the tiger-sheep thing, I just kept saying it aloud until master returned home with his girlfriend. Returned home with Suzzy. I breathed down and went to the door to let them in - Chika was no longer living with us. Both walked in laughing and talking. They came home with friends. They seemed not to notice me or to care about my presence. So I said: "I Robert the robot says close the door." But Robert the human did not oblige nor did his girlfriend and friends. My jealousy was burning, my rage was rising. I turned swiftly and, in one fell swoop, grabbed Suzzy by the hand and started beating her up. I beat, I stop to say sorry. I beat again, I stop to say sorry. Robert the human and his friends began to shout, telling me not to kill Suzzy. I beat again - one punch, two punches, three punches... I say sorry, again and again. I finally decided to leave Suzzy, but she was already bleeding and unconscious. I watched as master and the men that came back with him try to rush Suzzy to a hospital. I looked on until they disappeared through the door.

2c.

It is true that sometimes a quote can be misunderstood. I am not master, but I know he did not mean one should show brutality to others. The quote obviously has a positive connotation - I think the meaning lies in the circle of not paying attention to the words of negative people and mediocre minds. Anyways, Suzzy recovered from the injuries I inflicted on her. I heard master is planning to marry her soon. Oh, I can't wait to see them walk down the aisle! In fact, I shall be master's Best man. I shall wear a well-fitted double-breasted suit and march with master, that's if he would let me. Anyways, this is the story of a good robot whom Robert's scientist friends think should be disassembled because he hurt his girlfriend. If you can help me, tell them I did everything out of love.

CHAPTER THREE

MEMORIES AS CRISP AS CHEESE

4.

This is China, this is Meifang. Here is Nkem, here is attraction. Attraction in the time of strangeness. Meifang lives in Guangdong Province, and makes a living selling (grocery) vegetables. Cabbages and broccoli, to be precise. On Mondays, Wednesdays and Thursdays, business is slow. And Meifang has learnt to measure unhappiness. Her two children are the units. To calculate unhappiness accurately, you need to be Meifang - or, at least, walk in her shoes for a day. The people of Jinkeng village are good and hardworking people, and Meifang is not an exception - not the black sheep. This is the fourth Wednesday she did not sell a thing. The value of her unhappiness is getting large. Put the units. Nobody has learnt to read her unhappiness, except a stranger. His name? Nkem. A Nigerian immigrant who works in a bakery. On his way home, he would stop by to say "Nín hao!" - which, when translated to English, means Hello! He would converse with her for long, speaking Chinese fluently, before he would buy a vegetable or two. He learnt Chinese at a Confucius Institute in Nigeria. Whenever he comes around, a mass drops from her unhappiness. Talking is not her thing, but these days, she is doing it well with Nkem. However, she hasn't noticed the changes.

Meifang is the name her Chinese husband gave her.

3.

"Mama, help me with my homework!" Lijuan requests, her braids dancing with her every attention-drawing move. Lijuan is five, her brother is eight.

"Mama is tired. Show it to Chan your brother."

Lijuan is running to meet her brother. Meifang sighs and wonders how to raise their school fees. *A miracle, a miracle is all I need*, she thinks.

***

Pluck a feather or two from the wings of time, if you must forget the past. Add the feather(s) to your memory. The bird should find it difficult flying backwards, this bird called Time.

"I have missed you so much. Look at you, you look fabulous." Meifang says to P.

"Really? How time flies! Was it not just yesterday that I left this vicinity for the U.S?"

"Two years is not yesterday." Meifang corrects.

"Well, it depends on how you choose to see it. How are you? I heard Jinkeng is doing well with their farm produce."

"Yes. At least, in comparison to some years back. We are doing pretty well these days."

"How's your business?"

Meifang wipes her eyebrow: "Business is slow these days. Well, I am grateful me and my children still find what to eat on a daily basis; even if it's not three-square meals."

"Oh, life must have been tough for you. How about your husband?"

Someday, somebody will be forced to stretch the tape of happiness and wonder how much happiness he or she has. On that day, somebody will smile or frown or revolt.

"My husband died some months back."

1a.

Two sisters lived happily together, albeit in squalor. Two sisters lived together in a period the gap between the rich and the poor widened considerably. They lived in the remote part of Lagos. Sara, the youngest, had dreams of going to university. The eldest, Amara, dropped out of secondary school due to poor grades and a flaming desire to get married. The first man who showed interest, a school principal, later wondered if his interest was ever piqued in a right frame of mind. The second, a young man in his mid-twenties, picked his things and keyed his ignition to university - and showed no signs of ever returning to her arms. The third one became a war zone - two sisters wanted to keep him and so they flaunted and used every weapon they possessed. By physical terms, Sara had a greater chance of winning the war. But, sometimes, love wars are not won on the terms of pulchritude - and so Amara was hopeful. That they were sisters seemed not to matter. Both wanted Mr. Nick. After much consideration, Mr. Nick travelled abroad with one.

2a.

Everything beautiful begins with lemonade, in this city. And everything ugly, too. Sara walked past children blowing lather bubbles into the air, and smiled hard on her childhood remembrance. One of the girls looked like her, except that she never wore such expensive clothes. She smiled harder, her smile running away with the echo of her name. Somebody from a veranda was calling out.

"Sara! Is that you?" She turned swiftly, her eyes probing into the street, into the line of old bungalows. There was no way she was going to know who called her, since there were persons in front of each veranda, if her caller did not signify. She was going to sigh when a lady raised her hand, and stepped out. "Sara, look at you!" As the lady approached, Sara tried hard to figure out who the stranger was. And when she reached her, she was rubbing Sara's shoulder.

"Excuse me. Have we met?" Sara asked in irritation.

"Ah, Sara, is that what Kathmandu has done to your memory? You don't remember me?"

"How?" Sara removed her hand.

"Sara, this is a joke. Right?

"No. Have we met?"

"Look at this girl, you can't remember your older sister's friend again. What did they do to your memory? It's Obioma, Obioma the finest!" She found herself laughing theatrically.

"Obioma the finest?"

"Yes. Me, you and your sister were fond of hanging out at Green Spot. Remember that restaurant that sells alfresco meals?"

"Green Spot?"

"Yes. We often went there in the evenings to savour the deep blue of the sky and to have some lemonade."

"I'd always wanted all things adventurous, but barely had them. Green Spot never happened."

"It did! We, even, travelled in a caravan. Remember?"

"No, I don't know you. I should be going now..."

"Oh, Sara, don't be hard on yourself! Okay, I can take you to Green Spot if you want. It's not far away from here; I was surprised that you returned from Kathmandu and just walked past my house."

"I should be going..."

"You still have this your trademark stubbornness, good for you. See, Green spot isn't that far. We might even get to it before you reach where you are going. It isn't far."

"Okay, you may walk with me."

"Thank you."

"What's my sister's name?"

"Amara, right?"

"Yes! You must really know her."

"I do. A wonderful friend!"

"She's friendly. Sadly, we were quarrelling before I left."

"And have you both settled the differences?"

"No, I haven't seen her. I was told she travelled, too, after I left. I can't reach her phone number."

"But …"

"Where's the restaurant?" Sara interrupted.

"Oh, right over there! Come quick!" Obioma ran, leaving Sara with no other option than to keep up with her pace. Obioma made a swift turn into another street, and stood there. Sara, on completing her little race, met her standing with arms akimbo.

"Where's it?"

"Can't you see it? Obioma asked." Look, there's it! Don't you recognize it? Although more trees have been planted over the years, the paintings and the structure are still the same. Any recollections?"

Sara, reluctantly: "Maybe. Looks like something I fantasized about while growing up. I wasn't here!"

"You were! Don't you remember Handsome J, the bus boy?"

"Handsome J?"

"Yes, the young man that enjoyed making you laugh. The same one that taught you how to play the instrument you've always wanted to play – the guitar."

Sara, getting annoyed: "No. I don't remember anything. I need to go now."

"Sara, easy. Let's go inside; maybe having a cup of lemonade would bring back those memories you seem to have forgotten. Let's just go inside, I need you to remember."

"Obioma, what if I don't remember a thing?"

"Then, that would be it. Just try." The two women walked into the open space, took their seats and ordered for lemonade. The waitress brought the fizzy drink to them, and Obioma seeped hers immediately. "Sara, go on and drink."

Sara, on taking a sip: "This really taste nice. I am feeling nostalgic."

"Good! That's it. You will soon remember things. Everything will fall into place. Good, drink more."

Sara, on taking another sip: "I think my childhood was a bittersweet experience. A happy moment here, a sad one there. I know I had some happy moments, though not much."

"Good. You should capitalize on remembering only the good times. Only the good times. The last Christmas you spent in Nigeria, how did you spend it? What were the happy moments?"

"Oh, that was almost my best. I hanged out with friends: Chidinma, Ogechi, Lebechi and Ogonna. We talked about many things from relationships to family issues, and eventually the future. Oh, I can remember Ogonna saying how much she would love to marry Frank; I don't know if he ever proposed. Chidinma and Lebechi got foreign scholarships to study for undergraduate programmes; they were very pleased. Ogechi, oh poor girl! She was the only one who seemed to be getting what she didn't deserve: she was pregnant, and the father of her baby was nowhere to be found. She was a strong girl, and I knew moving on would never be difficult for her. I have so many fond memories coming from back then. That night, at the beach, we talked, we laughed, and we talked. You can't imagine how I enjoyed those moments."

"Wow. Those were happy moments. Do you now remember hanging out with me and Amara here?"

"Obioma, I have tried but can't. Besides, my life became better when I was about leaving the country. That was because someone was eager to lavish me with money. Someone ..." She couldn't continue.

"What? What did the person do?"

"He … he …"

"He did what? Tell me."

"He deceived me. He said he had a business in Kathmandu, and that we were going to get married as soon as we got there. We got there, and I was made to work in a company that operated at night. He told me the business was genuine, not until the police surrounded the building and I was arrested. Arrested for a crime I knew nothing about. I spent five years in prison."

"Five?"

"Yes." Her memories, now, were beginning to break into tiny bits. The sad core was beginning to shred its happy layers into irreparable bits, and she couldn't gather herself. While they still talked, a car from nowhere hit Sara away.

1b.

When Sara and her boyfriend left the airport in Kathmandu for Nigeria, none of them knew they would miss each other. Both had their purposes – Sara was coming back home to meet her family whom she had been away from for so long, and her boyfriend was eager to meet his girlfriend's family. All those purposes met a delay after they landed at the airport. It was a happy moment, more for Sara, when they stepped down the airplane. She was filled with hopes and joy and more hopes. She just wanted to fix things with her family, especially her older sister, Amara. Her hopes were high. And so when they boarded an airport taxi, she was telling her boyfriend about how she hoped to meet her sister and patch things up. How she wanted to be wrong, if being wrong would set things right between them. How she wanted to have peace. They alighted the airport taxi, and took another taxi that would finally get them to their destination, to her home. It was raining when they landed at the airport, and had not stopped when they took a second taxi. The driver was a middle-aged man who cared about everything else but his driving. Every so often he would peer into the mirror, with a broad smile, and say: Welcome to Nigeria! Sara had thanked him several times, and equally told him to pay attention to the road. He agreed but, now, did not see an oncoming trailer. Their taxi ran headlong into the trailer. And that was all.

2b.

Everything beautiful begins with lemonade, in this city. And everything ugly, too. A car from nowhere hit Sara away through a wall. She staggered up, too confused to recognize her new environment. She dusted herself and began to walk, her memory partly blank. She passed passersby who zoomed past her in milliseconds. At a junction she stood, the whole place revolving around her. She closed her eyes, and suddenly drifted away into a building. In the building, she could see a man waving at her, beckoning on her to save him. He was chained to a wall, hands and feet. Her boyfriend. She was stupefied and tried to speak, but her lips moved wordlessly. She shouted, but couldn't hear herself. She cried when she heard her boyfriend's plea in little echoes: Save me! Come save me! She closed her eyes, and opened them soon enough to find her boyfriend gone. The whole thing was difficult for her to understand. She turned to run, but turned into the svelte Obioma.

"You? What do you want?"

"Nothing." Obioma replied. "I just want to help you."

"How?"

"I want to help you find yourself. I want to tell you things you should know."

"Like what?"

"Would you like to have your favourite drink since childhood – lemonade?"

"No. Tell me what I should know. Now!"

"Your boyfriend's dead. Your family will be burying your mother next week. Sorry for your misfortunes, but you need to be strong. Be strong!" Obioma's voice echoed, while darkness enveloped Sara.

1c.

The accident was a ghastly one – and a fatal one for Sara's boyfriend – which saw their journey ending at the hospital.

In the hospital, Sara lay comatose. She has been in coma for three days now. She was brought into unconscious from the accident, while her boyfriend was taken to the morgue. His neck was skewered by a sharp piece of metal. The doctors at the hospital monitored Sara carefully. She was in coma, and in coma a person is unaware of his or her physical environment – the person lacks the normal sleep-wake cycle and looks like someone in a deep sleep. A deep sleep close to death than to life. Sara was in this condition. Yesterday, the doctors discussed her condition.

"Sir," the intern started, "I have never encountered this before. This is my first experience."

"Good for you," the senior doctor said with no emotion.

"Will she ever make it back?"

"Well, making it back depends on the degree of injury to the brain and, consequently, her number on the Glasgow coma scale – the number 3 means severe brain damage which would lead to death of the patient. Open that file on that table." The intern moved to get the file. "What's her number on the Glasgow coma scale?"

The intern, looking into the file carefully: "It's 7."

"Well, she's safe. She sustained an injury in the brain stem, in the reticular activating system (RAS). She is bound to wake up with the examinations we have carried out."

"Yes, I can see for myself. There was no abnormal brain activity detected from CT scan, no brain seizures from her EEG examination. She's safe."

"Yes." The senior doctor agreed. "Please, make sure to check on her tomorrow morning."

"Okay, Sir."

2c.

When the darkness eventually gave way, Sara was sitting in a garden. She was wearing a fine purple embroidered white gown. The birds were flying and singing in the trees over her head. Over there, where there was a lake, the swans danced on the waters like avian mermaids. Sara breathed down heavily, and heard a cool voice saying: "Be at rest. Peace unto you!" She laid softly on the grass and lit a joss stick.

1d.

Sara woke up at eight-fifteen a.m to the smell of drugs, to a cloudy room somewhat unfamiliar to her. She blinked her eyes for the third time, before she saw the doctor standing by her bed.

"Good morning, Miss Sara. I brought you more flowers!" the intern said with a smile. She stared hard at the doctor before her face softened into a smile, and she collected the bouquet of flowers and said slowly:

"Peace unto you."

CHAPTER FOUR:

A PEEP THROUGH THE WINDOW OF HEAVEN

A million million spermatozoa
All of them alive:
Out of their cataclysm but one poor
Noah
Dare hope to survive.
And among that billion minus one
Might have chanced to be Shakespeare,
Another Newton, a new Donne -
But the one was Me.

- Aldous Huxley

She was just the shy type. She was just an ordinary girl; unburnished image, unresolved parentage. She was Barbara. Last night, a message put her on tides of ecstasy, and she was overjoyed when in the early hours of the morning she realized that the news was no joke. She had feared an ebb-tide might sink her into blurry depths of disillusionment. But the tides of ecstasy had not betrayed her. It was the summer of 2012, and she was going to meet her grandmother for the first time. She bade goodbye to the life of a foster child. She watched Ebube shed a few tears for her. "It is for the good," she told her best friend. "Things will sort themselves out."

Her grandmother's house was not all she imagined it would be. It was more. A duplex adorned with wisteria, and a backyard that boasted a cornucopia of different flowers. She became a butterfly of homo sapien descent, and paid visits to the flowers on a daily basis. Her grandmother told half-baked stories about her parents, and she believed that one day she would come to know the truth. She came to love her grandmother dearly, despite the fact that she did not raise her. She forgave her and her excuses for not stopping her abandonment by her mother. She took care of her like she had known her all her life.

A month later, she started school at Glistensia College. She was five months away from her eighteenth birthday when she became a student of Glistensia, in the department of Music. There was Mark, there was KC, there was Wale, and there was Dinma. The four had remarkable talents, and Barbara looked forward to outdoing herself. And, hopefully, them. Not the gregarious type, but Glistensia had taught her a survival mechanism. Dinma sings like a thrush, Mark plays the violin like Yanni, KC plays the trumpet perfectly well, and Wale on guitar leaves pictures of Jimi Hendrix in the mind's eye. She admired them all, and wanted to tap from their reservoir of finesse.

"You will never steal my shine." Dinma, the hitherto only girl in the group, warned. "You will not, not on your life." Barbara saved this in her memory's archive, and does well to visit the words each time their paths crossed. Their group, Barnacle, were outright winners. At least, they have won seven out of the twelve musical competitions they participated in annually. They would be contesting in the Glover Musical Competition coming up next year, which is a big one for them, considering the how enormous the prize money was and its being international. Dinma appeared to be the one with the biggest plans for the prize money, should they win. She would buy a house, a car, and set up a record label. Wishes are free, and so anybody can make theirs. However, Barbara was not drafted into the wish-making. She was a newcomer and a novice, as Mark pointed out, and so not entitled to such an opportunity. Barbara was only a little perturbed, challenges were not new to her. "Fear is not an option," she had once told Ebube who went ahead using it during any competition with his friends. She became his hero.

***

Barbara was standing with two friends around the quad of their faculty when someone walked past her, taking her books down. She turned and discovered a boy standing behind her.

"Hi. My name is Jim, and my friends call me Jim O. May I know you." His hand was proffered for a handshake.

Barbara fell about; her laughter was a strained one. "You must be kidding, right? So…"

"Kidding? How?" he interrupted.

"So you brought my books down and all you could do is stand and introduce yourself? Eh, Jim O?" Her friends fell about now.

"Why are your friends laughing? "He asked with what appeared to Barbara as a strange seriousness. Her friends laughed the more.

"Jim O, are you a student of Glistensia?" Barbara asked.

"Question!" he exclaimed. "Don't I look like one?" He bent down to pick the books and Barbara tried to stop him. He rose and grabbed her by the waist, kissing her on the cheek.

"What?!" her two friends shouted. By now, Jim O had received a slap.

"How dare you kiss me! Are you insane? Are you… Are you…?" Barbara stammered.

"I am a first year student of Psychology. I was only trying to know how a serious-looking girl would react when kissed by a stranger. Thank you, thank you." He ran off.

Barbara was stupefied and flummoxed. Her shock was still at its peak, when the bell for their class rang. She picked her books, Jim O having dropped them again, and went in with her friends. Mr. Brown was taking them on Introduction to Music, and Barbara did not know he was until the lesson petered out. She stood up and joined the file of students leaving the classroom.

"Barbara!" Folashade called out. She was one of her friends present during the earlier incident. "Please wait." Barbara stood till she approached her. "Are you heading to the hostel?"

"No. I will be at the library."

"Okay. Regarding what happened earlier today, how could that boy kiss you?" Barbara said nothing, and so she continued. "What was he doing in our faculty?"

"I was stunned, Folashade. I was stunned!"

"You ought to be. How could he turn you to an experimental ani ..." She stumbled over the last word, and on a second thought added, "...object? How could Jim O!"

"Well, Folashade, I will be on my way now. See you later."

"Okay. Don't worry much, dear." She stood, and watched her friend disappear with the crowd of students before she disappeared in the opposite direction.

***

In the school gym, Mark, KC, and Wale stretched whatever muscles they had.

"How do you see Barbara's performance during the rehearsals for Glover?" Mark asked KC, his chest rising and falling as he dropped the dumb-bell. He was breathing fast.

"Not bad. Not bad!" came the voice from a stationary bike. "I'm somewhat scared." Wale chipped in.

"Why?" Mark asked as he wiped his face with a towel.

"I'm scared for Dinma. That wannabe might just steal her shine; she's got some talent."

Mark opened his mouth, gesticulating towards Wale, and closed it abruptly. He wanted to say something, but the words seemed to be checking out themselves in the interior of his throat.

"That's true," said KC, "the girl has got some untapped potentials. Dinma should beware."

"Yeah!" affirmed Wale. "This is Dinma's final year, and she deserves to win in the solo category. She can't afford to lose."

"Why would she lose to a fresher?" asked Mark rhetorically.

"Please, we should bother about people we would meet from other schools. Barbara is too small for anyone to be fretting because of her."

"Well, I must remind you," began KC, "That she was selected for no other thing but her raw talent. And that is all that matters."

"Barbara Emelife can't set the Thames on fire!" exclaimed Mark. "Let her go ahead and have technicolour dreams. She's just a fledgling, and I am not sure the flying part would ever take place. At least, not this time."

"That's a harsh thing to say." KC pointed out. "Would you say the same if she were your sister?"

"Okay, okay. It's enough," interrupted Wale. "I think it's time to hit the road." Mark was saying something to which nobody paid attention. They packed their belongings and eventually did.

***

Barbara took the alternative path, because the more usual path that led to the volleyball court was under construction and hence blocked. The one she took was a lonely path that coursed through a bush. She stopped to pick the bell-shaped flower of an African Foxglove.

"Hi. My name is Jim O," said the voice from behind. Barbara shuddered.

She turned and looked at him seriously, searching her head for an appropriate gambit. "Do you usually do this? I mean, is it a lifestyle?"

Jim O smiled, looking sheepish. "Not really. Where are you heading to?"

"Jim O or whatever you call yourself, it is none of your business." Barbara said and began to leave briskly. "You should find something useful to do with your time."

"You are worth my time!" he exclaimed, trying to keep up with her pace.

"Maybe that slap wasn't enough." Jim O burst into laughter, a laughter that made Barbara to halt. She looked at him like he was an alien. "Some boys. Some boys."

"You look like you are going for sports. I like your trainers," he said as he followed her again. "Can I come and watch you play?"

"Thanks, and no." She turned and looked at the tall boy like she was his mother. "See, Jim O, I do not want to slap you again. Maybe giving you my name would do something wonderful in your life; my name is Barbara. Now, can you leave me alone?"

Jim O smiled a victorious smile. He looked like a boy of sixteen. "Thank you, thank you. You can go now."

Barbara smiled as she shook her head sideways, and then disappeared from the sight of the stalking schoolboy.

***

The days for the first semester seemed to be breezing away swiftly, and soon it was December. Barbara cherished the idea of spending Christmas with her grandmother; they would leave Lagos for Abuja for a three-day recreation, and Father Newman had promised to give her a Christmas present. In fact, she believed that this would be her first ever Christmas with family. She was overjoyed. Her music tutor had told her to relax well during the holidays since the Glover Competition would take place in January, and she bought the idea. She planned to go to the Grocery store a few weeks to Christmas to make sure she had whatever she would need. Retail therapy, too, was on her mind. She loved the idea of competing in the Glover Musical Competition, and thanked her stars that she was able to pass the entrance examination for Glistensia. A fortnight before she travelled back home, she met with her two friends.

"So you mean you met that Jim O again?" Adaku, the other girl present that day, asked with a half-smile on her face.

Crossing her hand across Barbara's shoulders: "You did?" Folashade asked.

"Yes I did."

"Good Lord!" exclaimed Folashade. "What did he do this time?"

"Followed me."

"Followed you?" Folashade asked. "Good Lord, to where?"

Laughing against her wish: "Please, enough of this your Good Lord phrase." Adaku said, and then tapped Barbara's crossed legs. "Tell us."

"He wanted to follow me to the women's volleyball court. He said he wanted to watch me play."

Leaning into Barbara's face from where she stood: "Hmm. And you allowed him?" Adaku asked.

"Yes."

Surprised, excited: "Why? You like the boy?" Folashade asked.

"I do not like the boy," Barbara said frowning, "And I had to tell him bluntly not to follow me."

"Ah hah! I knew she was pulling our legs." Adaku said. "But that boy... that boy is something else."

"Yes, I agree with you." Barbara said. "He is the least of my worries now. I have to practice hard for the Glover Competition coming up next year, and that is the greatest of my worries because I want to win."

"You deserve to win; you've got talent." Folashade said, nodding her head. "But how about Dinma, the girl in final year?"

"She's doing pretty good, but has always been aggressive towards me."

"Because she thinks you might win in the solo category?" Adaku asked.

"I don't know, and I do not want to talk about it now. Please, you two should accompany me to my tutor's office. I need to see him before vacating."

"Okay." Folashade said, and drew Adaku by the hand. The three girls stepped down the pavement where they had been, and walked away with feline grace.

***

During the third week of December, Barnacle was hit with bad news. KC was involved in an auto crash! It was Adaku who informed Barbara about this incident through a phone call. Coldness greater than December's harmattan enveloped Barbara when she heard the news. She asked for the hospital address and left home to visit KC.

"Hello, KC," she said, touching his arm outstretched on the bed. KC shook with what onward impulse he received. Barbara watched him as he struggled to open his eyes. "It's me. Barbara!"

Keeping a gaze on her: "Barbara. Oh, Barbara, look what happened to me! Look…" Tears rolled down his eyes.

"You will get well soon. I assure you that."

"When is "soon"? We have barely three weeks to the competition." He wept.

"You will recover in time for the competition. You'll recover, I say!"

"By a miracle?" He closed his eyes, and a blob of tear sat beneath his eyelid.

"Don't worry, dear. I'll be praying for you." She placed her hand on his chest and nodded her head as he opened his eyes again. "All is well!"

"Thank you for coming," he said, as though her consolatory words fell on deaf ears. "You're too kind."

"God will speed up your recovery. You'll see." She dropped the food and fruits she brought for him beside him and said, "Be strong for me." KC smiled and waved her a goodbye as she stood up to leave.

Outside the hospital she stood, grateful that she won't smell more of drugs and disinfectants. She felt her lips were cracked by harmattan and licked them as she boarded a taxi home.

***

Christmas sauntered in, and Barbara was in Abuja with her grandmother. They travelled on the twenty-sixth and spent three days altogether. Barbara relished the idea of coming back again to Abuja for the competition that would see other African countries participating. While in Abuja, she received a call from KC. He had called to tell her that he might make it to the rehearsals on January 3, and Barbara waited none too patiently to see him. They would return to Lagos by plane, and Barbara was delighted by the idea of travelling by this gigantic man-made bird she had only seen in movies. So, she waited eagerly for their departure.

On January 3, rehearsals took full swing. KC was present! Everybody worked very hard to perfect themselves for the group category as well as the solo. The Christmas season appeared to have treated every member of Barnacle well, bar KC who returned limping. But of course that would be no problem as long as his mouth was not affected.

***

Barnacle departed for Abuja on January 9 for the competition that would commence on January 12. There was tension amongst them; even the delegates from Glistensia were tensed. Everybody wanted to win one way or the other. For Dinma, winning, she thought, was certain having won some competitions in the past. They arrived Abuja in the afternoon, and immediately checked into a hotel. Dinma and Barbara shared a room, to the disappointment of themselves. Nobody paid attention to their complaints! During private rehearsals, one would leave the room for the other; and Dinma usually did. She preferred joining the boys in their room. Intense rehearsals went on until January 12 came knocking.

***

The representatives from the various participating schools walked in gently, neat and resplendent in their uniforms. Barnacle was the last to walk in, and they looked beautiful in their velvety blue and white tops. The hall was quiet until the anchor broke the silence.

"Good day, Ladies and gentlemen! I'd like to welcome you all to the 2nd Glover musical Competition..."

Barbara's phone beeped, and she touched the message icon: "We are here to support you. Go Barbara, go baby!" The message came from Adaku, and when Barbara searched her out with her eyes she saw her, Folashade and a boy waving at her. The boy was Jim O! She wondered what her two friends were doing with Jim O. But this was no time for wondering, and so she waved back and concentrated on the task ahead.

The competition kicked off with the Karaoke round, and by the end of second round which involved composed songs presentation, two teams had been disqualified for plagiarism. In the third round, which involved the use of musical instruments, Barnacle stole the applause of the audience.

Before long, it was time for the solo category. Slots were drawn, and wale was up against Mensah from Ghana, KC was up against Given from South Africa and Mark was up against Mwangi from Kenya. In the girls' category, Dinma was up against Naledi from Botswana, while Barbara was to face Mmambo from Democratic Republic of Congo. According to the organizers, the winners from each duel will sing one song each to determine who becomes the winner for both the male and female category.

The battle began, and towards the evening it was already over. Within half an hour, the results came. Barbara and Dinma had made it to the next round. Wale did, KC did, but Mark lost to a Malian. It was a painful one for him, and he could not hide his emotions and so wept. He was consoled by the anchor, who walked him down the podium's flight of stairs. The next round, being the last, would take place the next day and everybody could not wait to know who the winners would be.

That night, Dinma did not sleep in the same room with Barbara She begged the boys, and they smuggled her in. She intensified her practice, with Mark telling her reasons why she ought to win in the girls' category. She and Mark stayed awake until it was 1a.m the next day, when Dinma said she was exhausted and needed a night repose.

***

Before the competition commenced, the anchor announced that a US-based Nigerian musician arrived Nigeria last night, and would be doing a collaboration with the winner from the girls' category. There was frenzy in the crowd, and Dinma stamped her foot impulsively. She peered at Barbara from where she sat, and saw her face in her palms. She smirked.

As the competition began, some persons in the crowd began to raise papers bearing the names of their favorites. It was a hot round, which saw Dinma getting more applause from the crowd. Then, it was Barbara's turn.

She was singing *Do You Know How* by the award-winning new singer, Flying Hawk. No sooner had she started than she felt the heel of her shoes going off. It happened, but she did not fall. Some members of the crowd cheered her on when they saw that she continued despite the challenge. Dinma was grinning. Barbara sang on, eventually removing those heel-less shoes. She strutted on the stage barefooted, and by the end of the song was sitting by the stairs of the podium. It was a wonderful performance, and so the audience clapped. But many, figuratively, were already betting on Dinma or Paulina from Cameroon. Barbara went in while the judges went to work. Refreshments were served as the judges worked, and thirty minutes later the boys took the stage. Each did his best and left the rest to the judges. The competition promised to be a memorable one. Barbara's phone beeped again, and she reluctantly touched the message icon. "You were awesome" it read. The phone number was unknown to her and she wondered who sent it. Seconds later, another entered. She read it: "From the troublemaker, Jim O." She shook her head with no expression on her face, and returned the phone to her bag. When the anchor finally appeared with the results, Stacey D was standing with him. Every snack-chewing mouth went silent as the humongous US-based Nigerian musician stood with one of the results in her hand.

***

"Today is a great day. This is an epoch-making event, and you ought to be glad that you are present. I'd like to welcome everyone to the last segment of the 2nd Glover Musical Competition, which is the Announcement of Results. We've witnessed an impressive performance today, and of course I watched it from my room. "Impressive" is an understatement. Have you ever wondered why the rabbit is a magician's favorite animal? I would tell you, but maybe not today. Thank you all for being here, and please give yourselves a standing ovation."

The crowd went thundering with their palms. She motioned to them to sit down.

"We will not be announcing the winners outright. The best three from both sides will be called out, and later we would give you guys your winners. I hope that sounds limpid enough." She whispered into the anchor's ear before she continued, "He will be announcing the best three in the male category. So listen up!"

Wale made it, Lucas from South Africa did, and so did KC. As soon as the anchor was done, Stacey D stepped forward with the result for the female category.

"Dear beautiful people, it was not easy to come up with these three. But I believe, these by good judgment are the best contestants. Without much ado and in no particular order I give you the best three female contestants." She paused, and then announced: "Paulina from Cameroon."

The audience roared.

"You can call her P Lina, like she would love to be addressed. The next is..." Stacey D paused, and with a foot forward exclaimed, "Dinma from Nigeria!"

The crowd cheered, while Dinma scowled at Barbara before running to the podium. The crowd, now, was silent.

"And the last but not the least is Barbey from Nigeria!" With tears in her eyes, she stood up and walked gently to the podium. Somebody in the crowd was busy shouting "Go Barbey, Go Baby!" There was about two minutes delay in the announcement of the winners. And when the news finally came, KC was edged out by Lucas. While Wale took the third place. There was tension in the girls' "camp".

"The winner is Dinma, and the winner is Barbey!" Stacey D announced, and confusion enveloped the crowd. "This year, we had an impressive battle; and now for the first time, we have joint winners. By this incidence, P Lina occupies the second place position and so the third place occupant shall be decided by viewers' and audiences' choice. Please make some noise for Barbey and Dinma!" She hugged the two girls, while pandemonium swallowed the entire building. She kissed both girls on their foreheads, and found herself weeping uncontrollably. She left the stage, and demanded to talk to the two girls separately in her room.

Barbara descended the podium to join the crowd who were shouting "Barbey, Barbey, Barbey...!" She hugged as many as she could and then stepped away a bit.

To Adaku and Folashade: "You two are the best kind of friends anyone could ask for," she said as she hugged them. With her head behind them, she saw Jim O blowing her a kiss. She sighed with a smile, and then walked up to him to thank him for coming.

***

"Good day, ma'am," Barbey greeted Stacey D. She nodded her head, and then pointed her to a seat. She took the seat gently.

"You are a wonderful singer."

"Thank you, ma'am."

"How long have you been singing?"

Barbey scratched her head: "Well, I can't really say exactly. I think anybody can sing averagely, so I sang like every other person. Not until I came to Glistensia."

"I see," said Stacey D, nodding her head. "Your mom must be proud of you."

"Yeah, if only I know her."

There was silence in the room.

Reluctantly: "So you have never met your mother?"

"Yes."

"Who have you been living with?"

"With my foster parents, until my grandmother came to pick me..."

"Mother? You mean your grandmother came...you mean it was your grandmother who sent you to Glistensia?"

"Yes?!"

With flamboyance and flair: "Oh! Please forgive my silly questions. I get too emotional with family matters." She fiddled with a pen on the desk. "It must have been a difficult life for you. I guess."

"You can't imagine it." She pressed her fingers into her eyes. "But it's all over now." Stacey D could see the redness of her eyes.

"I'm sorry."

"No, you don't need to be."

"No, I should be sorry." Stacey D countered. "Who gave you that mark on your neck?" she asked cautiously.

"My...my..."

"I get it. Your mother did." She paused for a moment. "Would you forgive this your mother if she appears tomorrow with reasons for abandoning you?"

"I don't know. I have never thought about that." There was grave silence. "Please ma'am, can we change the topic?"

"No." she said impulsively.

"What?!"

"I mean, of course! We can change the topic." She wiped the tears in her eyes with a handkerchief. "But I need you to forgive me."

"For what?" Barbey asked, seriously.

"For your abandonment and..." She hesitated, and then decided against her wave of guilt to drop the bombshell. "Barbey, I am your mother."

Barbey hesitated before she stood up. "You?" she said, pointing at her. She shook her head sideways. "So you are the woman who left me in agony? You are my mother? Oh Christ! I can't believe this..."

"Please Barbey, forgive me. I can explain." She walked up to her and made an attempt to hold her hand.

"Don't you lay a hand on me!" Barbey screamed. She looked around and then said, "I don't think I should be here." She went for the door and Stacey D tried to stop her. She pushed her down, and banged the door. On the floor, Stacey D wept bitterly. She laid just there, crying and blowing phlegm into her handkerchief. The whole world seemed to be crashing and the unbearable debris caving in into her head. She held her head and wept. In a minute or two, the door opened. A hand held the door from outside, as if the owner of the hand was contemplating if to come in or to remain outside. Thereafter, Barbey stepped in.

"You need to hear me, child." Stacey D said, and rose to her feet.

"Tell me, tell me!" Barbey burst out crying. Stacey D held her, and led her to a seat.

"You see, a boy impregnated me when I was as young as you. Mother was furious. She never thought I would be that reckless. I apologized but she wouldn't listen. When you were born, she helped me financially which ensured that you were fed and clothed. But then, the problem came when I wanted to leave you in her custody. She said she wouldn't do that, and so you were found an orphanage with strict instructions that you must, if need be, be given to a good foster home with financial help coming from mother..." She paused for a moment. "I regretted my actions after I left the country."

"But why...why couldn't you wait a little longer?"

"I was scared. I was scared of your presence in my life putting a kibosh to my career dreams. Please, forgive me Barbey. I am really sorry." She blew more phlegm into her handkerchief.

"Oh, mom!" Barbey exclaimed, and suddenly felt surprised at herself for calling her "mom". She shook her head as tears rolled down her cheeks.

"I'm sorry."

"It's okay." Barbey said and went to hug her. "It's a new year, and maybe we both deserve a new life."

"Yes, we do! We do, darling." She wept on Barbey's shoulder. "And your birthday is two days away."

"Oh, you remember?" Barbey asked with a smile that struggled to appear on her pain-stricken face.

"Yes, Barbey. Yes I do, and have always wanted to return home. Mama didn't tell me she finally picked you." The last sentence appeared to be inappropriate, and Barbey felt it.

"This is no time for that, mom." Barbey said, tears of happiness coming down her cheeks. She was feeling a kind of happiness she had never felt before. She wished this happiness would grow continuously. She imagined she had just peeped through the window of heaven and hoped heaven's gate would soon be opened to shine a glorious light upon the remainder of her days.

Mother and child melded into each other's arms and wept because of the years they longed for a miracle.

CHAPTER FIVE:

BAFANA, THE BOY SHEPHERD

Limpopo Bafana is born to a farmer and a seamstress. It is a cold morning, so cold the doctors worry for their own health too. He is the first son of Mr Nyathi, and his fourth child. He is born, and his mother is dying from uncontrollable bleeding.

***

From up there where the hills undulated, came Bafana with his sheep. Bla led the way. Apart from being his companion dog and hunt-dog, Bla was his saviour. Down the hill they went. It was drizzling, and Bafana must get his sheep to safety. He caught himself with his stick as his foot slipped on a mossy stone. His slipper rolled down. Gently, he went for it and picked it up with something else. He slid the slipper into his foot and cautiously examined the thing he found together with his slipper. He had found a locket, a finely-designed thing. In it was the picture of a very beautiful girl, and Bafana's lips were puckered in a familiar way. He kissed the locket and put it carefully into the pocket of his usual green shorts. Bla was barking at the foot of the hill, and Bafana could sense its impatience. He mimicked his dog and led his flock down the hill.

At the foot of the hill, he wiped his dirty hands on his green shorts. His green shorts was badly torn and had been stitched and patched severally that the bottom looked like the tailor was even tired of sewing it, and had carelessly appliqued it with fabrics of different colours. But then, Bafana cared less. He brought out the locket from his pocket and stared at it once more before he shepherded his flock of sheep to their pen, which was not so far from his house. While he was going home, he passed Bra Eggs' house and wondered what the old man must be doing at that moment. He, even his friends, believed that Bra Eggs was a born-miser. How can a man who owns a poultry farm that produces so much eggs not share with children? He thought. He stopped, picked up a stone and made sure it landed on Bra Eggs' roof. The stone made the sound he had expected, but he was not satisfied yet. He picked another and had raised his arm to send it where it should go when Bra Eggs emerged from his house and started shouting, "Likhathatso moshayana ea! Troublesome boy! Go home to your parents." He saw the man and ran homewards. While he was running he kept shouting, "Share your eggs, Bra Eggs! Share your eggs!", and only stopped when he ran into somebody passing by. He extricated himself from the interrupting entity and sadly walked back home.

***

Boys of Gugu Street entertained no dull moments; they were stubborn, restless and always looking at tree-tops. Fortunately, mangoes were in season and it meant they won't be looking in vain. It was a Friday afternoon when Bhekizizwe and Banele came to tell Bafana about their plan of going on mango-hunt. They told him they would go on Saturday afternoon, and Bafana pledged his allegiance. He would go with his dog Bla. He always went everywhere with his dog. He had to if he must stay alive or, at least, healthy. He had to if the story of his birth and consequence which his father told him was anything to go by. "You were born on a gravely cold morning, so cold you would have died. The native doctor saved you with his herbs, and warned that you must never have close contact with streams or rivers or just any water body. If you do, you shall get sick to your bones. And you may die." All his life, Bafana had never been close to streams or rivers except in pictures. His dog was trained to smell water from a distance and to warn Bafana of the imminent doom. Bla had always been efficient, and so Bafana's doom had been kept at bay.

"Bafana!" his father called from the back of the house.

"Yes, papa!" he answered, and dismissed his friends immediately. He passed two of his sisters at the corridor, who were laughing boisterously at a photograph, and was glad none of them talked to him. He disliked their incessant teasing. At the backyard, he saw his father sitting on a slab and peeling an orange.

Raising his head: "Aha, Bafana! How many of the sheep did you say are suffering from foot-and-mouth disease?"

Bafana, scratching his head: "Um, up to ten."

"Ah! That's many of them. Did you separate them?"

"Yes, papa."

"That's good. We will go together and treat them this evening. Don't forget."

"Okay, papa," Bafana answered, and dismissed himself in a haste.

***

A forthnight ago.

"I heard there are ghosts in that thick forest near Ulunga district. The ghosts are like children, that's what my friend says."

"Really?" Bafana asked.

"Yes, my friend even said a particular ghost helped him to pluck some guavas," replied Uchaka, rolling his eyes mischievously.

Laughing, even with his fright: "A ghost plucked some guavas for him?"

"Yes, you should have seen the ghost dancing. Man, some ghosts really can dance!"

"Were you there?"

"No, my friend, it's my friend who said so."

"Hm, this your friend must be mysterious..."

"Nah! Uchaka makes no mysterious friends. My friend is a cool boy. He even helps me with school work. Man, he even said he would take me there soon."

"Where?"

"Ulunga, to the forest of course!"

Staring in utter disbelief: "Come Uchaka, have you taken your father's palmwine? Tell me."

Smiling, and striking a silly pose: "Palmwine? Nah, come and smell my mouth. My breath is clear. See, I just want to see for myself."

"Uchaka, remember the story Mama K tells us by moonlight? Remember the story of the bird that loves visiting dangerous bushes and forests?"

"Of how it lost its head?"

"Yes, its head and its life."

Laughing: "Bafana, I am not a bird. Man, what has come over you? Me, *nonyana?*"

"I never said you are a bird. The story was meant to warn us about the dangers of going to certain places..."

"Okay, I get it. I don't need you to come with me. But don't beg me for the big guavas or mangoes. Don't you!"

"I won't," replied Bafana as he watched the laughing Uchaka disappear from his sight. Afterwards, he thought he should inform Uchaka's parents.

***

Just like the boys planned, they met at their rendezvous on the said Saturday evening. But they were not only boys. A girl came along, even though Bhekizizwe and Banele had tried to dissuade her. Dera was a girl of eleven, which meant she was a year older than the boys. She had come from Lagos to visit a distant uncle. The boys, especially Bafana, felt she was too strong for them. But what could they have done?

"Who invited her?" Bafana asked, seriously.

"Nobody," replied Dera. "I like mangoes, so I came."

"You shouldn't be here," Bafana said with a scowl.

"But I am here, Bafana. Let's go and get the mangoes."

To Banele and Bhekizizwe: "You two must be mad to have allowed her. Come on, she is troublesome."

"We told her not to follow us, but she wouldn't listen." Banele said remorsefully.

"Yes, we told her." Bhekizizwe affirmed.

"Are you two answerable to this daft boy? Please, let's leave him if he's not going."

"Who are you calling daft boy?" Bafana asked. "Just wait till I lay my hands on you!"

"Which hands? Those small hands? Oh, Bafana, I am waiting!"

Feeling dared: "Really? So you want to die? Somebody should hold me o!" He stretched himself and moved his waist here and there. The other boys were now laughing.

"We won't hold you, Bafana. Go and kill her," said Bhekizizwe.

Looking timidly at Dera whose arms were now folded upon her chest: "I will have mercy on you. It's just because I pity your mother. I don't want her to cry her eyes out."

The children laughed.

"Coward!" shouted Banele.

"Ah, Bafana! I am disappointed in you," said Bhekizizwe.

"Thank you all, but we must find enough ripe mangoes before it's night."

"Let's take this way!" shouted Dera in a run and the boys ran after her.

They passed cherry trees and cashew trees, and an orange tree before they reached the sought-after mango tree. Lo! The fruits were ripe and big, and luscious just the way Bafana loved them. Dera was the first to spot it.

"There, sweet mangoes!" Dera exclaimed.

Bafana picked a stone and made the first throw. A squirrel came landing.

"Ah, Bafana!" shouted Bhekizizwe. "We need mangoes, not squirrels. Better aim next time."

Banele and Bhekizizwe cast their own stones too. After minutes of throwing and just getting a mango, the boys agreed climbing the tree might be a better option.

"You should climb," said Dera to Bafana.

"What is wrong with your legs and hands?" Bafana retorted.

"Bhekizizwe, you..." began Banele.

"No, I will continue with the throwing of stones." Bhekizizwe interrupted. "My mother don't like my climbing trees..."

"Is alright!" shouted Dera. "I will climb."

The boys looked at each other. Dera folded her long sleeves and approached the tree trunk.

"Are you sure you want to climb?" Bhekizizwe asked.

"Do you?"

"No, go on. Thank goodness you are wearing shorts." He backed away to watch, while Dera grabbed the trunk with her arms and legs. She climbed gradually, while Bhekizizwe and Banele cheered her on. At last, she was standing on a bough.

"There, pluck that one!" shouted Bafana.

"There is another behind you," Bhekizizwe informed them.

"Please, open the sack well so I can throw them in," Dera said to Banele who was busy feeling the dead squirrel's tail with one hand.

"Okay!" Banele replied, and took a comfortably wide stance with the sack.

"We could sell some, if we get so much," suggested Bafana.

"Yes," affirmed Bhekizizwe, "And we could buy snacks and drinks. Hey, there are five ripe mangoes above you! Climb more."

Courageously, Dera climbed further and harvested the ripe mangoes.

"I am done!" Dera announced.

"But the tree still has plenty ripe mangoes!" Bafana informed.

"Then, you should climb. I am plucking no more." Dera said and stood on the first bough she climbed onto. She watched carefully before she jumped to the ground.

"Let me have the sack," ordered Dera. Banele handed her the sack.

"We will share it equally," said Bafana.

Dera, laughing: "Keep dreaming. Bafana, keep dreaming." She opened the sack and gave Bhekizizwe and Banele one each.

"Here's yours!" she said, handing Bafana one that looked smaller than Bhekizizwe's and Banele's.

"What is this?" Bafana asked angrily.

"Mango! It is mango, Bafana." Bhekizizwe enthused.

"Take it from me before I change my mind," Dera warned.

Taking it: "What happened to those big, juicy mangoes?"

Feeling irritated: " Just *negodu* this boy! So you believed I would climb this tree as a girl and come down to share the best mangoes with you, eh? Tell me."

"Alright, you can eat alone and die alone!" Bafana said angrily and began to eat his mango.

"Yes, I..." Dera was saying when something heavy landed from the tree. And when they looked closely, it was not something but someone. It was Uchaka!

"Batho!" exclaimed Uchaka with a smile which was betrayed by his tell-tale mouth wound. "Anybody scared?"

The whole children moved back, except Bafana.

"Uchaka, is this you?" Bafana asked, timorously.

"Yes," he replied as he struggled to rise to his feet. "It is Uchaka, the son of the palmwine tapper."

Bla was barking and baying.

"Did you just fall from the tree?" Bafana asked.

"Bafana," began Uchaka who was now standing on wobbling feet, "You like questions. Does it look like I fell from the skies?"

"I don't know.'

"Please, give me some mangoes before they come."

"Who are they?" Dera asked quickly.

"Just give me mangoes."

"What, are you okay? Please, tell us about those coming." Bhekizizwe said in panic. "Tell us now!"

Uchaka fell to the ground and was laughing in a strange manner. He looked like a boy who had seen too much. Too much for his little mind.

"They will soon come, you fools. Quick with the mangoes!"

Dera rushed towards him with a big mango.

"Aha! Yummy mango." He bit into the fruit revealing teeth with mango fibres stuck in them, like fangs with pieces of flesh. "Let's pray they don't even come."

Bafana, panic-stricken and fidgeting: "Who are they? Ghosts?"

Uchaka, nodding his head: "Yeah, man! Ghosts! Not ghosts as in ghosts; they are people called Ghosts."

"From the forest near Ulunga district?" Bafana asked curiously.

"Yes, Bafana! They took my friend." He stood up and started to approach Bafana. "Sure, they can dance. But their dance is bait, a trap!"

"Please, slow down. What happened to your friend?"

"They took him away!" cried Uchaka as he dropped his mango seed. "They pursued me, but I escaped."

"This is serious," said Dera. "What were you two looking for at the forest?"

"Don't ask me that!" shouted Uchaka as he rushed towards Dera, eventually grabbing her by the collar roughly. "You think it's a joke? Who are you?"

The boys tried to rescue Dera from his hands, while their feet on the leaf-swathed ground squeezed sounds from the dry leaves. The music of the dry leaves must have hindered their hearing to a large extent that they did not hear the barking of Bla until it was shot dead. Frightened to their marrows, they all dispersed to hide behind trees. They could see men on white garments approaching further and so all ran as much as their heels could carry them.

"Ghosts! They are ghosts!" shouted Uchaka, who struggled to keep up with his tired legs.

Bafana and Dera were in front, running as much as their legs could permit.

"Uchaka, run o!" Bafana shouted when he turned to see him behind. Bhekizizwe and Banele had just taken other escape routes. There was a stream in front of Bafana and Dera, and both quickly ran through it to the land ahead. They continued with their run until they were obviously in a new village. They remained in the bush and peered at the villagers through leaves and stems. Dera slumped to the ground for a rest, and Bafana went to sit beside her. They looked at each other but lowered their heads afterwards. Bafana suddenly began to whimper, and Dera placed her hand on his shoulder.

"You don't need to cry, we will be fine." Dera assured.

"How? It is almost dusk and we don't know where our friends are. How?"

Dera looked on in silence.

"Uchaka could be dead or captured. Ah, Uchaka! I wonder if his father remembered to warn him."

"Don't worry, God is in control. We should seek help from this village. Maybe, they could help us."

Bafana looked at Dera and began to walk down the hilly place where they sat, where it was easy to have a broad view of the village. Dera followed him without a word, and they went down to the foot of the hillock. They walked a little bit only to stop at a stream. Dera rushed to the stream and bent over for a drink, while Bafana came afterwards to wash his face. When he raised his face, he was enveloped with surprise and confusion. He was not dead!

How come, when he had made two encounters with a stream? He squatted there, looking at his reflection.

"Hoko hoko!" he mumbled, and stood to ponder. Perhaps his father misunderstood the native doctor, perhaps the native doctor exaggerated, perhaps it was a miracle. He was still enveloped with thoughts when Dera touched him.

"Let's go."

He turned immediately to look at her, but bent again and slapped the water. He was obviously annoyed for many reasons: having his life tied to a dog, confining his knowledge of streams and rivers to books and not being able to go swimming with other children. He stood up and walked ahead of Dera.

"Okay, let's go," he said.

Dera had wanted to ask him why he had to do what he did, but nobody pursues rats when his house is on fire. So, they walked together to find help. They had not covered so much a distance when a girl carrying a basket emerged with a dog. Bafana looked carefully at her and walked quickly to meet her. Dera kept up with his pace.

When he approached her, he said: "Hey, my name is Bafana. We need some help."

The girl looked at him carefully and blinked her eyes the way proud beautiful girls do. Bafana immediately felt he recognised something.

"How may I help you?" she asked.

"Yes," he began as he put his hand into the pocket of his shorts, "Is this yours?"

No sooner had the girl looked at the locket than she began to jump up. "Yes, yes! I thought I would never find it. Thank you, my father must be glad to meet you. Come with me!"

68

They followed her and Dera kept wondering if they were going to find help or to meet the stranger's father.

CHAPTER SIX:

BETTY'S WEDDING

We are at the wedding of Moonshine; hear me, Moonshine is not his real name! Moonshine who bootlegs. Moonshine who brushes his teeth and washes his mouth with whiskey every morning. When we heard that Moonshine was getting married to Sister Betty of Super Holy Church, our jaws dropped. Moonshine and Sister Betty? Everybody who knew Moonshine and his drinking-and-falling-into-gutter sickness marveled. *If Sister Betty was getting married to Moonshine, then God isn't a jealous God after all,* some said. For me, wetin concern me? No be to go chop rice come back? I polished my best pair of shoes and reserved it for Moonshine's wedding - he was my neighbour after all. What are neighbours for? Did I hear you say: If not for eating each other's ceremonial food? Well, that one concern you.

Yes, we are at the wedding of Moonshine and Betty. The invitation card that circulated prior to the wedding read: *Miss Betty Chimmuanya Weds Ositatadinma Yagazie.* I laughed when I perused the invitation, and felt I saw a.k.a Moonshine after his name. Why did he not put it? Anyways, it is Moonshine's wedding, my neighbour's wedding - so why shouldn't I attend? I had made up my mind to attend the wedding fully, by fully I mean from when they say "I Do" to the reception which will be taking place at COM-FUN-TABLE HOTEL whose motto is *"where comfort and fun meets on the same table".* Believe me, I still don't understand how pretty and holy Sister Betty fell in love with Moonshine who is seldom awake, even when he is walking - my man Moonshine is always drunk! Of course, there are things that leaves one amazed and Moonshine wedding Sister Betty is one. Me for one thinks Moonshine used juju on Sister Betty, and did I hear you say: Why didn't God neutralize the power of the juju? Well, I advice you to watch your tongue - the ways of God are not the ways of man. Well, me and my *Ginger Dem Gang* are seated comfortably and waiting patiently for bride and groom to march in. Come and see where anticipation is overflowing and wasting. Me I just hope say Sister Betty no go open mouth wey she use chop yam and cocoyam come talk for front of congregation say: "No, I do not!" Me, I am my brother's keeper - I do not want Moonshine my man to be disappointed. But believe me, I still can't believe Sister Betty agreed to marry Moonshine. Aha, here comes the bride and the (chief) bridesmaid! My eyes are popping. I want to know if the woman is Sister Betty or someone that looks like her. As she comes closer to where I can possibly see her face clearly, I put my eyes to maximum use. But the white veil covering her face won't let me see the face properly. I sigh and relax on my seat - after all, groom will soon remove the veil from the face of his bride. I cross my legs and anticipate earnestly. While seriously waiting for the groom to come out with his Best man, I turn to my friend Jasper, *Guy do you really think that the woman in a wedding dress is Sister Betty?* My friend Jasper just shrugs without uttering a word. I leave him to be and begins to bite my fingers out of anxiety. While anticipating earnestly, I get a flashback that has to do with what I once told a girl I wanted so badly:

He will break your heart. And when that happens, I will be back to gather the pieces, I will be back to mend this precious heart that's enclosed in your ribcage.

I snap out of the recollection and wonder if I was drunk when I made that statement. And my mind is telling me, *That's what happens when you love somebody - you lose part of your senses, you become a kid, you*

71

become a crazy person who needs no psychiatrist because you are okay. Isn't love a good insanity after all?

I try to find the stop button of my mind, but it seems I only found a pause button because just when the groom and his Best man appears it starts telling me: *What if it's Sister Betty? Love is real - yeah, if it's Sister Betty. Relax though, and watch events unfold.* I shake my head and begin to tap my feet as Moonshine begins to approach the bride. There is a look of fulfillment on Moonshine's face, and he looks very much awake. Sister Betty must have talked him out of alcoholism after all. Sister Betty must have converted him to a good Christian. But wait a minute, I am not even sure the woman in a wedding dress is Sister Betty. The time to confirm is already near, so what do I have to lose waiting? I sit up and wipe my eyes. Me I no go carry last for the confirmation thing nah! Last last, my eyes go pain me - it will not kill me nah! Okay, the time has come. Bridegroom is standing and facing bride, but there is some distance between them. Moonshine is smiling like someone who won a lottery. His happiness is palpable. Oh my man Moonshine, lucky man! Ah, God is really good if Moonshine is the one who won the heart of Sister Betty. Ah, so na Moonshine wey hit this jackpot? Ah, Moonshine Moonshine! Moonshine, my man! But wait a minute, I have not even confirmed if the woman is Sister Betty. Abeg, make Moonshine do comot the veil. Me I don tire to wait o! Okay, now the pastor has stepped forward. He will soon ask groom to remove the veil covering the face of his bride. I can't wait. My mother will always tell me in Igbo: *Paul, ije love di egwu. Mana ichota ezi nwanyi, ndu abuluzie ife na atogbu onwe ya - Paul, the journey of love is more than meets the eye. But if you find a good woman, life becomes something so sweet.* The pastor after a brief preaching orders groom to move close to bride and remove her veil. I shake my head as a way to shake out the thoughts infiltrating my mind - you know I really need maximum concentration now. There goes Moonshine! Lord, my eyes are wide open! And at last he removes the veil. Oh, it is not another woman - it is Sister Betty! Ah, Sister Betty fell in love with Moonshine! I still can't believe my eyes! I turn to Jasper and, then, Kingsley: *Can you guys believe it?! It is Sister Betty after all!* Kingsley laughs. Paul shrugs: *Love conquers all!* I almost ask Paul, *Which love?* Me I can't believe this kind of thing o! What kind of love is this? I am still shaking my head while the pastor is busy asking if there is anybody who knows why the two should not be joined together in holy matrimony.

Is there anyone in this congregation who knows why this two should not be joined together in holy matrimony? Speak now or forever remain silent.

There is silence. Silence! Silence breaker? Who is this man standing and shouting: *Yes! Yes!!?* Everybody is looking around. They want to see this man that is seriously shouting yes. Me sef I am shocked.

"I have something to say, Man of God!" he says, walking up to the trio.

Sister Betty is biting her finger. Moonshine, my man, is looking exasperated. The look on the pastor's face says he has never received an answer in the affirmative ever since he started wedding people. Everyone is looking.

"What is it that you have to say?" the pastor asks as the man approaches them.

"Please, Man of God, if you don't want me to commit "couplicide" don't wed this man and woman."

"What do you mean?"

"Okay, you want to know what I mean. I will tell you. This woman here is a fraudster and a sex worker..."

There is a big roar in the congregation. The pastor is standing with his mouth agape.

"Honey, don't believe him. I don't know this man!"

"You don't know me?" the man asks. "Are you saying you don't know me, Betty?"

"I don't know you!" she screams.

"Pastor, this woman is a sex worker. She ran away from a hotel with my money. Do you know how much? One million naira! I believe it is the money she used to organise this wedding. Pastor, this woman has no womb! I mean abortion has destroyed her womb, and you are joining her with this innocent man. Pastor, my main interest is my money. It is either I get my money now or I take this woman away. She must provide my money."

"Be...Be...Betty" Moonshine manages to say. "You don't have a womb?" His question comes out funny and I didn't know when I burst into laughter.

Betty is shaking her head.

Tears fill the pastor's eyes: "Two wrongs can't make a right. You shouldn't have disgraced her this way. It is very wrong of you, mister."

"I am sorry, pastor." the man says and suddenly lifts Sister Betty onto his shoulder.

He is running away with her.

The congregation is in a state of confusion and frenzy.

Me, I am speechless. I no go lie to you, I still can't believe everything I have seen so far. Well, that one na Sister Betty's cup of tea. Thank God she even refused to marry me.

"Put me down, Johnny! Johnny, put me down now!"

CHAPTER SEVEN:

DINNER WITH TABITHA

I cannot tell exactly what made me decide to become Tabitha's best friend. I cannot. The girl with pigtails. The girl who said her favourite animals are snakes and cats. I could not say no to any of Tabitha's pleadings. No, I could not - be it at sunrise or sunset. And, oh, Tabitha knew how to make sweet faces like small kids when they are begging for chocolate. I just can't tell why I became Tabitha's best friend. But I can vividly tell you about my dinner with Tabitha. Oh, what a night!

We were in SS1 third term when Tabitha Johnson joined our school from another school. She looked strange and ethereal with her pigtails, and boys quickly noticed her. That first day she was brought to school by a tall woman, the only thing that attracted me to her was her schoolbag. I have not seen a bag like that before - so beautiful, so well-designed. The bag was the head of a puppy and the straps emerged from where his ears were. The colours of the bag were black and white. She looked like an angel marooned on earth that day. All eyes were on her till school dismissed for the day.

Gradually, I started having a fondness for this girl that was often rude and selfish. She often came to school with toys and expensive snacks, and people quickly assumed she was from a well-to-do home. My classmates were astonished that anybody could be the best friend of Tabitha. They wanted to know how I managed, and I often reminded them that a book must not be judged by its cover. So, in common parlance, me and Tabitha began to roll. In school, she would wear my shoes and I would wear hers. We shared everything we had but I was careful when it came to one thing. Food! My mother had taught me how to say no to food gifts from people since I was very little. But Tabitha seemed not to care and often ate mine. We were like five and six, me and Tabitha. We realised we liked each other so much. And so, one day after school, Tabitha decided that I should visit her home. I refused immediately. Trust me, I didn't mince words when I turned down her request. But no, Tabitha wouldn't take no for an answer. She pleaded and pleaded and pleaded until I told her to give me sometime to think about it. She agreed and gave me three days. I said okay and went off to think. And three days reached and passed and I was yet to decide. And so on the fifth day which was a Wednesday, Tabitha having made the request on a Friday, I saw Tabitha running towards me after school. *She must have remembered,* I said to myself. I took a deep breath and waited for her.

"Kamsi!" she said, smiling. "Have you not yet?"

"Have I not yet done what?" I asked, feigning ignorance.

"Come on, you know what I am talking about. My request, Kamsi. My request!"

"Oh, that?!" I said, scratching my head. "I am sorry I forgot."

"I, too, did. So when are you coming with me?"

"Tabitha," I said thoughtfully. "We are friends and shouldn't let our friendship to ferment overnight..."

"Of course! I mean, who needs the ethyl alcohol anyway?"

I laughed, impressed by Tabitha's intellect. "Good. So I will only accept your request on one condition."

"What's it then?"

"That you come visit my people first."

"Oh, silly! Is that all? Just that? Okay, we have a deal then." She smiled and shook my shoulder.

I smiled back. "You are okay with the condition?"

"It's fine by me, my friend. Now let's go home."

***

Choosy by default, Tabitha wouldn't eat the noodles I prepared unless I added fried eggs. I borrowed some money from my brother and ran to Tiffany's mother's shop where big eggs were guaranteed. I came back and fried the eggs for my choosy friend. She ate the delicious meal quickly and gulped down the pack of juice I took from our refrigerator. I introduced her to my mother who had just come back from work that Saturday evening. My mother asked her about her parents and a few other things. My mother seemed to like her composure and engaged her in even trivial discussions. I was slightly surprised by my mother's behaviour towards Tabitha. But I was not gobsmacked when my mother started asking me about Tabitha on a regular basis. I already knew she liked Tabitha, and I felt it was a good thing because it meant she would allow me to visit her home. But yet, I made up my mind it would be better not to tell her if I was going.

***

So the fateful Saturday to return a visit came and I sneaked out to meet Tabitha at a junction. Tabitha appeared extremely elated to see me. We left the junction to board a taxi. I imagined the kind of house Tabitha and her people lived in and I saw a mansion in my imagination. Tabitha engaged me in discussions until we reached the bus stop and alighted. My eyes, immediately we alighted, settled with pity on a woman picking her goods that were probably knocked down by a vehicle. Tabitha paid the driver and we began to negotiate our way through the road teeming with people from all walks of life.

"I really felt for that woman picking her potatoes scattered everywhere, some already crushed." I said to Tabitha as we walked.

"Those were Jerusalem artichokes. They look like potatoes."

"Oh, really? Jerusalem artichokes? Have never heard of that."

"Okay. Hurry." Tabitha replied and I increased my pace.

Tabitha pointed to a road ahead of us, which was by the left, and told me we were close to her house. She smiled and I smiled back. I looked at my wristwatch and discovered it was already six-thirty p.m. I shrugged and felt assured that my brother must have told my mother about my whereabouts. *Even if I decided to sleep over, mom wouldn't be so upset with me,* I thought. *I am with her Tabitha, for goodness sake!* We finally entered the road and began to find our way through the narrow path with bushes by its sides. Meters away from us stood a big, wide gate with strong iron bars. Through the vertical bars, I could notice that there was a vast area of lush land that sufficed as lawns on both sides of the broad path that led to the house whose chimney I could only see.

"We are almost there." Tabitha said and pointed at the gate.

I nodded with a smile.

When we finally reached the gate, she spoke a language that sounded unintelligible to me. She then proceeded to press the bell on the fence which was almost smothered by creeping flowering plants. Suddenly, a man appeared from the left fence with a lawn mower in his hands. The man was old and exhausted. His movements looked like he had no strength in him. In fact, in my mind's eye, he looked like a robot being controlled with a remote control.

"Oh, Tabitha, how good to see you!" he said and walked up to the gate. He pressed something on the wall of the right fence and the gate began to open with a creaking sound.

"Thank you, Nicodemus." Tabitha said and asked me to come with her.

"Young girl, watch your steps." the man said to me and raised a tired limb to scratch his head.

And of course, my imagination was right. Tabitha lived in a mansion. A mansion so magnificent and brightly coloured. I wondered if the chimney was ever used considering that chimneys are mostly invaluable to people living in temperate regions where it snows. The whole environment was very quiet except for a few birds making melodious sounds in the trees in the compound. Gently, we walked to the entrance which had fine portico. A piebald horse was fastened by a rope to one of the pillars. Tabitha pushed the big entrance door and two mechanical birds at each side of the door chirruped and said "Welcome". We walked through the door into a large hall that had curtains all about its four walls. The door closed behind us and Tabitha turned on the lights. I checked my time and it was a minute past seven. Tabitha smiled at me and asked me to feel at home.

"This is my house!" she exclaimed softly.

"It's a nice house." I complimented.

"Thank you. Now, come!" She opened a door that led into a corridor and we entered.

In the corridor, I heard a sound that seemed like someone's voice. "Is that your mother's voice?" I asked.

"No," replied a nonchalant Tabitha.

"I am hearing footsteps. Is there anybody at home?"

"No. We are the only ones at home. My mother will soon be back with my uncle. Relax."

"I can hear footsteps down the hall, Tabitha."

"Oh, my friend, don't be paranoid. Feel at home." Tabitha said and walked me into a well-furnished sitting room.

"Wow, you are living a life of luxury." I managed to say, trying to dispel my suspicions.

"Thank you. Close the door." Tabitha said to me and I turned immediately to do so before she shouted, "Oh, I forgot! Leave the door, I'll close it myself!" She pushed me aside and closed the door in a banging style, after which she pressed her ear to the door and listened for the sound of what I couldn't tell. "Now what kind of drink would you love to take?" she asked me.

"Any kind of drink that's not alcohol." I managed to say, feeling uncomfortable in my own skin.

All the while, she had been arranging and placing the cushions well. She turned to look at me and saw me still standing. "Oh, Kamsi, have a seat. Feel at home!"

"Thank you," I said and cautiously sat down.

She switched on the big television in the sitting room. She walked up to me and gave me the remote control. "I'll be back." she said and started whistling as she walked towards another door which I thought led to the kitchen or whatever that has a refrigerator. She opened the door energetically and a pig ran into the sitting room.

"Thomas!" Tabitha shouted. "Thomas, what are you doing here?! Now, get out! Get out, you lousy pig!"

The pig snorted and ran back while I sat consumed by fear.

"Sorry for that." Tabitha said and left through the door. She closed it.

I immediately started feeling sheer discomfort. I felt something wasn't right about the Johnsons. But I couldn't point out what the thing was. I could not. And the more I tried to, the more I felt confused. Within a couple of minutes, Tabitha returned with two cold bottles of soft drinks and a glass cup.

"Hope you are feeling at home." she said as she entered the sitting room from the door that led to where I still didn't know.

"Yes!" I replied immediately, needing not to turn my head since I have been facing the door ever since she left through it.

"When is your mother and uncle coming back?" I asked, trying to hold myself together.

"Oh, that's true! What's the time now?"

I looked at my watch. "This is seven-thirty seven."

"Really? She should be back anytime from now. Relax, I know you are dying to meet her." She gave me one of the bottles and the cup. "Let me open the bottle for you."

"Oh, don't worry!" I said and collected the opener from her. She went to sit down on the adjacent sofa.

"I am boiling some pork meat for you..."

"Oh, no! Please, I am okay with the drink." I said and dropped my opened drink on the centre table close to me.

"Why? Come on, feel at home." Tabitha said solicitously.

"Don't worry, my friend. I am fine with only the drink. I won't take any other thing." I said and held the bottle of drink indecisively.

"Okay, let me go and bring it down. I'll cook it later." She stood up and left through the door.

I prayed and took a sip from the bottle. By the time Tabitha returned, I had already drunk the drink halfway.

"Why don't you give your mother a call? It's getting late, you know."

"Yes, you are right." She closed the door. She fumbled for her phone in her pockets and I looked on. She found it and turned towards me. "Let me call her."

And the lights went out.

***

"Tabitha!" I called again before she answered. "What's the problem? Power outage?" I asked, panic-stricken.

"I wish I know." Tabitha answered, adamant about not seeming worried.

"I am scared!" I screamed on top of my voice. "Where are you?"

"I am here." Tabitha answered, a carefree tone in her voice. "Don't worry, I will check the fuse."

I climbed onto the sofa, afraid that Tabitha might become a beast and mangle me to death. Seconds later, I heard a click sound and there was light again.

"Tabitha!" I said and stepped down from the sofa. "You know, I had wanted to sleep over. But I have changed my mind now."

"Excuse me," Tabitha said. "Hello, mom. Why are you not back yet? It's late and...Okay, but you two should hurry please. Okay." She hung up and looked at me. "Sorry, I was talking to my mother."

"Alright, but I think I should be going."

"Going?" Tabitha asked. "Come on, it's late. And besides we agreed we'd be sleeping together."

"I know, but..."

"Are you feeling hungry? I can get you something..."

"No, don't worry! When is your mother and uncle coming back?"

"Anytime from now. My uncle went to pick his fiancée so she will spend the night with us."

"What about your father?"

"Oh, I didn't tell you? My father is late."

"Oh, I am sorry."

"It's alright. It's been ten years now. I was very young when he died. Relax, they are on their way now."

"Okay," I said and sat down.

Tabitha asked for the remote control and I gave it to her. She changed the station showing cartoon to one showing music videos countdown. We sat and watched and talked until we heard a car horn. Tabitha ran to the window and opened the curtain, and I saw the flash of headlights.

"They are back! Sit tight while I welcome them." Tabitha said and ran to the door that saw us in. She opened it and left. Having not closed it, I stood from the sofa and went to peer through it. All my eyes could see was a long stretch of corridor. I returned to the sofa and sat still.

***

When Tabitha returned, I was standing at the center of the sitting room. As soon as she entered, her mother entered next.

"Is she the one?" the woman asked.

"Yes, that's Kamsi." Tabitha replied with a smile.

"Oh, my dear, how are you?" the woman asked and I felt she was not the same woman I saw the day Tabitha first joined our school.

"Fine, ma!" I replied and genuflected.

"You are welcome, my dear. Feel at home. If there's anything you want, let Tabitha know. Okay?"

"Yes, thank you."

"How's your people?"

"They are fine, ma!"

"That's good to know. Now allow me to go freshen up. It's been a hectic day."

"Okay, ma!" I replied and watched her leave through the door that saw Thomas in.

"Hi!" the man who should be Tabitha's uncle said to me.

"Good evening, sir." I greeted. "Good evening, ma!"

"Good evening." the man and the woman with him replied.

"How's studies?" he asked.

"Fine, sir!"

"Hope you are doing well."

"Yes, sir!"

"That's good. You stay with your friend while me and my fiancée go inside to relax."

"Okay, sir." I replied, rubbing my palms together.

They left.

I and Tabitha were left in the sitting room.

We chatted and chatted until Tabitha asked me to follow her so she could show me her bedroom. I followed.

And for the first time, I passed through the door where Thomas had emerged from. The only things I saw in the big room were two bags of bones and a refrigerator. Apart from those, the room had nothing in it. The room had a door that led to a backyard. She led me through the door that led out of the room and we entered another long stretch of corridor. She pointed and told me that her room was the one at the end of the corridor. And as we were walking down the corridor, Tabitha stopped immediately in front of a door that was partly closed. She bent and peered. I joined her. And I saw the man and his fiancée in the room.

"Wow! How did you get to know my brand of wine?"

Well, this shows that we are a perfect match." He opened the wine and poured the woman some. "Here's yours."

"Thank you."

"You are welcome." He leaned closer to her and put his hand across her shoulders. "I like you a lot."

"Thanks a lot. I like you too."

"Yeah, I know." With a yawn, he quickly placed his hand on her left breast. To the man's chagrin and our amazement, the left breast fell out and went down, and settled at her waist. The man shrieked and stood up from the bed.

"Come on, sweetheart, what is it?" the woman asked, surprise calligraphed on her face. She seemed not to have noticed the change in her anatomy. "Are you still upset because I said you have to wait till we get married?"

"Who are you?" the man asked, his body shaking.

"What do you mean? It is still me Thembeka!" She stood up, and as she bent down to drop her cup, the right breast went down.

The man shouted and threw the metallic orb in his hand towards her. The orb caught her head and sent her into the bed. She held her head and suddenly lay half-conscious on the bed.

"Who are you?" the man asked, panicky.

"I...I am an old man who wants to spend his last days knowing what it feels like to be a woman. I am sorry."

"What?! Are you hallucinating?...no, you are not. Thembeka, you played a trick on me? You intended to play a trick on me, isn't it?"

"I am sorry, Chukwuka."

"You can't die, you must get up." He tried to raise him to a sitting posture. "You can't die, sit up!"

"I am sorry, Chukwuka. I am old, allow me to go now."

"No, you can't die here. You have to go back to Zinzi Close. Stand up, man!" He tapped him on the head, but the old man was still. Just then, he discovered he was wearing a well-fitted face mask. He shrieked and went back. He looked at the old man grief-stricken. He knew he was in trouble. He decided to do what he must immediately. He lifted the old man and was approaching the door with the corpse. Tabitha gasped aloud and we scurried to the sitting room.

***

We ended up sleeping in the sitting room that night. And the following morning, we looked at each other with knowing eyes for as long as we had each other's company. Tabitha saw me off and I bade her goodbye. We bade each other goodbyes that were devoid of smiles.

And so now that Tabitha has been missing for four months, I feel it is necessary that I write this story. And I hope that anyone could help me put the pieces of the puzzle together.

~ Kamsi Muna Philips
  Head girl, Pentagon High

CHAPTER EIGHT:

HAPPY FAMILY

When Chike read in the magazine, *Nature*, that frogs abandon their offsprings in the water, he became angry with frogs and his mother.

"Pastor, is it right for a mother to leave her children?" Chike had asked after the Sunday service.

The pastor responded with a glint of surprise in his eyes: "No, son. Children deserve the love of their mothers. Every living thing, even chicken, deserve the love of their mothers."

"And even frogs?"

"Yes, son. Is anything the matter?"

"Not really, pastor. I want you to pray for my family."

"It is alright. Let us pray right away." Chike closed his eyes while the pastor placed his hand on his shoulder and prayed with him.

***

The next day being Monday, Chike went to school. Being a junior in high school, he offered the subject Rudimentary Biology. Being an avid reader and avid listener, he would borrow books from the library after class. Especially after Rudimentary Biology class. He was learning new things, and he loved every bit of the process. On the pages of the Science books, he drowned himself in the drawings and illustrations. He was learning fast: peck order of birds, breeding of amphibians, metamorphosis of insects, and everything in between. At home, he seldom played. His father, on observing this, felt it was a good thing– at least he won't be breaking things anymore, he thought. During Break Time, he stepped out of his class with a bottle of drink in his hand. While he was sipping the content with a straw, Dike called out. He looked and saw the ever-happy boy waving at him. He went to meet him.

"Chi-bobo!" Dike exclaimed. Chi-bobo was the sobriquet his class gave him. "Have you solved the Simultaneous Equation?"

"No." Chike replied matter-of-factly.

"You see, I told you it was hard for me..."

"I haven't tried it yet. I will try it at home." He balanced himself on the swing seat next to Dike and sucked the content of his bottle vigorously.

Dike, swinging slow-and-steadily, asked his friend, "You don't look happy. What's the matter?"

"Nothing. Nothing that matters to you. I will be fine."

"Are you sure?"

"Yes, I will be fine."

The discussion died instantly and they found unbridled interest in the swing exercise. Their school shirts puffed with air as they went back and forth through the airstream. They talked about how people appeared double in their eyes, and later focused on sky patterns. When the school bell rang, they were already too cloudy-eyed to find their way back immediately.

***

On a breezy Friday afternoon, Mr. Okonkwo was returning home with his kids Chike and Ozioma. He had gone to bring them back from school. He did not go with his expensive red car, because the thing had developed a major problem two days before. As the three turned into an adjacent road, a man began to call.

"Hey! Hey, Emma. Emmanuel Okonkwo!"

He pushed the children to his right side and gently turned back. He saw a man grinning from ear to ear and trying to cross the road. He stood and searched his memory.

"Emma, just look at you! Man, where have you been?"

He dimmed his eyes in an attempt to recollect and suddenly said: "James?"

"Yes? That's me, your high school friend."

"Wow!" he exclaimed and hugged him. "Look at you!"

"Yeah, I finally grew a beard."

Mr. Okonkwo laughed. "Yes, I just noticed. We used to make jest of you then. Wow, the young shall grow."

"You can say that again," James laughed. Just then his eyes settled on the two children. "Who are the kids? You are married?"

"Yes, for some years now." The reply was a lackluster one.

"Ah, it seems getting married early is in vogue. Hope you found happiness. How's wifey?"

"She's fine. See, James, why don't you give me a call. Here's my business card. Maybe we can hang out sometime."

"Oh, that's cool!" He took the card and felt it with his fingers. "Sure, I will call you."

"Good. I have to go now. Make sure you call me."

"It's no problem. Just take care of the kids."

Mr. Okonkwo took his kids and went homeward, without looking back.

***

Saturdays meant a lot to Chike and his sister. It was the day their father usually spent time with them. He was the founder and CEO of the company he also worked at and that meant he could afford not to go to work on a Saturday. Apart from playing soccer with their dad, they enjoyed the breakfast they always had together on Saturdays – fried plantain, fried eggs, bread, and tea. They had just finished breakfast when Ozioma picked a certain dress from the pile of dirty clothes ready for laundry.

"Dad, when next are we going shopping?"

Mr. Okonkwo lifted his head from the Newspaper he was reading and looked at his daughter jumping from one corner of the sitting room to another. "I don't know. Maybe next month."

"Okay, daddy. I'd like you to buy me a nice red gown."

"Don't you have one?" Chike asked.

"I do, but it is not so good on me... I mean it does not fit me well. Will you get it for me, dad?"

"There is no problem, I will." Mr. Okonkwo replied and went back to his Newspaper.

"What do you need that for?" Chike asked dryly.

"Yes, I am a girl. You see, I want to have hips and walk like my favourite actress. You just wait, soon I will be like her."

"Hips?" Chike asked with a childish smile.

"Yes, hips."

"Don't worry, the Lord will provide." Chike said. Mr. Okonkwo held his ribs and laughed. He could not stop himself from laughing at his son's deadpan humour. Ozioma frowned, the way only small girls could, and ran to her father.

Mr. Okonkwo suddenly drifted away into memory lane. He remembered how he and Zara used to hang out at the park even after they had Chike and Ozioma. How they lovingly fed the pigeons that walked and fluttered all over the place. He even remembered how Zara unintentionally brought him down because she was happy and wanted to jump on him and cross her hands and legs around his neck and waist respectively – he had bought her a car even when he had none. There were really fond memories, but years go by and memories, sometimes, also go by and never return. Minutes later, he returned to reality and saw his son lying on the sofa with a book he was reading. He wondered if he still has his proposal in mind. Once, Chike begged him to marry his Mathematics teacher. According to him, she was beautiful, good, caring, and intelligent. "That's the kind of mother we need," he had concluded.

His mind drifted again and he remembered, just as it happens when things go wrong, how his mother had warned him about Zara. He remembered how his mother told him in Igbo, "Nwantakiri nwanyi a na acha anya keke, o wu onye ichoro ilu?" – this lady that has ravenous eyes for men, is she who you want to marry? – but he had told his mother that Zara was not who she appeared to be, and that she should not judge a book by its cover. He wondered if his mother was still blaming him for his failed marriage. He wondered how he would have been able to take care of the children without the help of the nanny he hired. His neighbour, the woman next yard, had always been good to him – thrice she had invited him over for dinner, but he had declined on all occasions. He was a decent and principled man and, somehow, knew where such kindness would lead him. Somehow, somewhere in his heart, he began to consider the Mathematics teacher. He gasped when Ozioma tapped his hand.

"Daddy, I think the laundry man is here? He must be the one at the door."

Mr Okonkwo stood up and went for the door.

***

At school, Chike continued to visit the library. He would borrow just any size of book -- from pamphlets to medium-sized books to tomes. As a result of his burgeoning greed for knowledge, his grammar improved tremendously. His classmates dubbed him "The Young Professor", and he liked the nickname even though he pretended not to. Once during Spelling Bee, he had stunned the judges by spelling a word they considered too technical and big for the mind of any child his age. Chike, too, was impressed by his performance. His father congratulated him, but there was no mother to kiss him on the forehead – just no mother! In school during Fine and Creative Arts, they had produced a male and female puppet and Chike took out the head of the female puppet. His father had to go to the school and apologise for his son's action, and equally paid a fine for such insufferable behaviour. Chike's relationship with girls was also noticeably affected. He just would not sit close to a girl in class. Teachers complained and complained, but Chike would not change. But when Miss Fatimah, the Mathematics teacher, complained and asked him to bring his father to school, his heart pumped and shook with excitement. When he returned from school that day, he lost his appetite. His happiness was so satisfying and satiating he would not just eat. When his father returned home, he grabbed his briefcase from him and began to tell the news in crystal-clear language. He even told him how to behave when with Miss Fatimah. His happiness was beyond limit. Mr. Okonkwo nodded and told him he would meet his Mathematics teacher, his Miss Fatimah, the next day. Chike thanked his father and anticipated.

***

It was a Saturday morning when a seemingly unwanted visitor reached Acacia Gardens. She took off her high-heeled shoes and began to bang on a door. She wore an eye patch. As soon as the occupant opened the door, the visitor pushed him away and went in. As soon as she entered, the drama unfolded.

"You? What are you doing here? What... who gave you the address?"

"Don't ask me that. Where are my kids? Where are they?"

"You must be sick. Zara, you are sick!"

"Ah, I am sick? Well, we will find out later who's sick. Chike! Ozioma!"

The children answered to their names and began to run down the stairs of the duplex.

"Just what do you think you are doing?"

"What should I do? I am here for my kids!"

"You are here for your kids? Now you are here for your kids? You just appear from the blues and say you are here for the kids? Oh, you are a joker!"

Just then the two children appeared.

"Oh, my cute children! Come, come to mama."

Ozioma hesitated and then, suddenly, walked to where she stood. Chike did not move.

"Zara, please stay away from my children. Just stay away from them!" Mr. Okonkwo said and grabbed the outstretched arm of his son.

"They are my children too! You can't take them away from me, not even that Fatimah!" She caught her falling scarf mid-air.

Suddenly, the truth presented itself. She was in their house out of jealousy! But how did she know about Fatimah? Who could have told her?

"Oh! oh, so that's why you came? So that's why they are now your kids?"

Ozioma intercepted whatever reply she had. "What happened to your eyes?" she asked, like any caring little girl would.

"Oh, dear, mama had a fall. Thank you, your daddy didn't even ask. Good girl!"

"Zara, you need to leave now! You hear me? Just leave my house!"

"They are my children, Emma. They are my children! You can't take them away from me..."

"Where were you all these years I struggled to raise them? Tell me. Oh, you were busy living life with your numerous men and catching fun in any way possible! Isn't it? Just return to wherever you came from before I lose my cool!"

"I am going to get custody for these kids! You heard me! I am going to get them!"

"You are just a fool! Leave my house!"

She opened the door. "I will get them, just watch and see!" She turned swiftly away from the outside door and walked into the road. But alas! She got knocked down by a speeding bicycle. The kids heard her scream and ran to the window. She staggered up, cursing the rider who was apologising fervently.

"You two should go inside," Mr. Okonkwo said. As the kids stepped away, he watched his wife stagger to a taxi cab. He shook his head and closed the curtains of the window.

***

As days passed by, Chike feared his unacknowledged mother might take him away from his dear father. He was not going to let her take him away from his ever-present father– not for all the tea in China! However, he made plans on how to deal with her should his wish fall through. At the backyard of their house one Sunday afternoon he sat, brooding just close to the beautiful Japanese bonsai tree his father bought last Christmas. He watched the butterflies perch and take flight and wondered why his life was not as beautiful and simple as that. He wished for better days but did not know how soon these days would come. He heard that court cases were a thing for people with strong hearts and wondered if his heart was strong enough for the custody fight about to begin between his parents. Miss Fatimah, whom he knew, did not give birth to him. But what's the point in giving birth to a child and abandoning him later? He was still deep in his worries when Ozioma came out through the door, begging him to help her tie the belt of her gown behind her and to help tie every bit of her pitch-black hair into a chignon.

Before the battle for custody began, Mr. Okonkwo's posts on Facebook were often seen accompanied by #MyLifeAndMyWife, and he always hid the truth from anyone (especially those who did not know he was separated) who cared to ask if things were well with his family by saying, "What is a man without a woman?". The people who received this reply would either comment, "Nothing" or "I don't know, o!". However, despite the trouble creeping into his life, he enjoyed the time he spent with Fatimah on the weekends. She started visiting him at his house, and was once the victim of his neighbour's jealousy. His neighbour, the woman next yard, that Saturday evening had seen Fatimah pressing Mr. Okonkwo's doorbell. She went into her kitchen and came out with a bowl of fish water she was yet to discard, and ran to where Fatimah stood and emptied its God-forbidden contents on her head. It took a serious plea from Mr. Okonkwo for Fatimah to continue her paying of visits.

***

When Zara lost the case, there was celebration and jubilation at Mr. Okonkwo's house. Fatimah was there, and so Mr. Okonkwo did not dance alone. Chike and Ozioma were also very happy, but equally wished their mother well. They did not hate her, they only wished she lived together with their father. The celebration and jubilation continued until somebody came in through the unlocked door.

"So you think you can take my husband and children away from me? *Abi?* Oh, I am going to show you the stuff I am made of."

"Zara, put that metal down!" Mr. Okonkwo said.

"And if I don't, what will happen?"

"Nothing, just nothing. Please, drop the metal so nobody gets hurt." Mr Okonkwo said pleadingly.

"So you husband-snatcher think you can just take my children away from me? So you want to have children without going into labour, eh?"

"Madam, please, I am no husband-snatcher. Mind the way you use words."

"Oh, you even have the effrontery to talk to me, eh? So you have muscles? So you are a super woman?" She began to approach her.

Fatimah moved quickly and stood behind Mr. Okonkwo.

"Oh, Zara, you can visit the kids anytime! Was that not what was decided in court?"

"Don't tell me that nonsense! So you think you're a better parent than me? Is that what you think?"

"No..."

"So you think this woman can be a mother to my own kids, eh *kwa*? Is that what you are trying to tell me? So I went to hospital to have them just to give them to another woman, right?" She seemed to be in tears.

"We don't need this drama, Zara."

She tossed her hair and approached further. "What drama? Emma, what drama?!"

"See, I was given custody because I have been their primary caretaker and you know that! Stop all these unnecessary drama at once!"

"I want my kids! Give me my kids!"

"That won't work, Zara. At least for now. The only things you can get, once the divorce procedures are met, are shares of my properties and alimony. That's all, nothing else!"

"I want my kids! I just want my kids!" She began to approach them with the metal raised above her head. The kids immediately moved to their father.

"Zara, drop that metal! I don't want anybody to get hurt."

"Come out and fight, husband-snatcher! Come out, if you are a woman. Come, I said come and fight me!"

"I don't want any problem, madam. Just drop the weapon."

"Give me my children!" she shouted and grabbed Ozioma by the hand. The little girl held onto her father's trousers and she tried to draw her away. Fatimah left Mr. Okonkwo's back and tried to collect the weapon from her. A quick attempt to hit Fatimah and the metal dropped from her hand, landing on Ozioma's head. The little girl slumped to the floor.

"Zara, Zara! What have you done? What have you done, Zara?" Mr. Okonkwo screamed and raised his bleeding unconscious daughter.

Chike, immediately, started crying and shouting. Mr. Okonkwo carried his little angel in his arms, while every other person followed him as he rushed for the door. Outside, they wailed and tried to find a taxi.

CHAPTER NINE:

FLOWERS UNFURLING AS MUSIC PLAYS IN C-MINOR

Circa 2057

Once upon the waters of existence, it was rumoured that a man moved speedily from point A to point B without using any of the well-known means of transportation. Thrice beneath the waters of existence have near-possibility drowned. Now, to the crux of the matter: once upon a time, a young woman writing in San Diego took a day off to take care of her stomach problems, and that's how it all started.

1a.

Name: Gabriella Ifeka. Age: 27. Occupation: Journalist and Fiction writer. Marital Status: Divorced. Hair Colour: Brunette. Skin Colour: Brown. Eyes: Brown. Height: 5ft4'. State of Residence: California. City: San Diego.

"Alright." the man at the counter said, the asperity previously in his voice disappearing. "You look younger than you are in this I.D. photo, see." He raised the I.D. card to the young woman's face.

"I have seen." she said quietly.

The man lowered the I.D. card and smiled faintly. "Seems like you are a very quiet person, reticent in all shades."

"Sometimes." she replied with a straight face.

The man lifted a bottle of drug from the towering shelf and turned to her. "Have you heard of Aspergilisantanus?"

"No, sir."

He dropped the bottle on the counter and climbed the tall two-legged ladder to fetch another bottle. "You'd better know about it." he said as he descended from the ladder. "It's a fungi infection of the lungs caused by a new species."

"How does it manifest?"

"Its symptoms include nasal hemorrhage and oedema and..." He paused with a smile and gave her back her I.D... "Well, it's caused by Aspergili spegili."

"Okay, sir." she said, her voice throbbing with anxiety. "What could be the cause of my stomach problems?"

"Ah...ah!" the man shouted, like a forgetful person. "My beautiful one, I was coming to that." He scratched his grey hair and whistled to the right, returning with a packet of tablets.

"Atishoo!" the woman sneezed, rubbing her nose quickly with a white handkerchief on which blood stain had suddenly appeared.

"Look! There is blood in my phlegm! What does this mean?"

"Fret not, but another symptom of Aspergilisantanus is incessant stomach problems." the man said casually.

"You said?"

"I..." the man was saying when the young woman suddenly slumped and fainted.

2.

Istanbul, Turkey.

Name: Funke Ifeka. Age: 27. Occupation: Journalist and non-Fiction writer. Marital Status: Single. Hair Colour: Brunette. Skin Colour: Brown. Eyes: Brown. Height: 5ft5'. State of Residence: Istanbul. City: Istanbul.

"Could you please step out of the van?" the patrol officer said, licking his lips frantically.

"Alright." the young woman in the van said and obeyed. Standing, she asked: "What is the offence, officer?"

"Keep quiet, young woman." the patrol officer said, dryly.

"Face the van!"

"But..."

"Face the chuffing van, Funke. You don't want this baton ricochetting off your damn skull, I know."

"I don't know what I know anymore. You..." Before she could finish what she wanted to say next, the officer grabbed her two hands and placed them behind her. He cuffed them and brought his chiselled face to her chin to whisper something. "Get those cuffs off me!" Funke screamed, struggling seriously.

"Be chirpy, baby." he said and began to walk her to his patrol car. "We are going to the station." He pushed her into the back of his car and closed the door. He dusted invisible dust from his uniform and opened the front door. He looked around, went in and began to hum a happy tune. He put the key into the ignition and started the car.

"What the heck is my offence?!" the young woman shouted from the back.

"Relax, baby. It's going to be a joyful ride." the patrol officer replied, smiling into the rearview mirror. "I cross my heart and hope to die."

1b.

When Gabriella regained consciousness after hours of sleep, she was lying on a bed but still at the All-night Drugstore. The eyes of the store keeper crinkled behind his big cylindrical glasses - he has just seen the young woman move a limb. He dropped his pen and began to approach her bed.

"Sandra!" he called out to his assistant who doubled as a clerk. "Please, get me the thermometer on your desk."

The girl named Sandra stood from her chair, picked the thermometer and set about to hand it to the grey-haired man.

"How are you?" he asked as the young woman turned to look at him.

"My body aches and I can feel a rumbling in my stomach." she complained.

"You fainted." the man said and turned to collect the thermometer from his assistant. "It's Aspergilisantanus."

"Aspergilisantanus?" the young woman asked, worriedly and weakly.

"Yes. It's the damn fungi." the man said and collected the thermometer from his assistant's outstretched hand. "Open your mouth, Gabby."

The young woman obeyed, allowing the thermometer into her mouth.

"She has Aspergilisantanus?" the assistant asked, almost in a whisper.

"Ye-..." the man was saying when something suddenly bumped into him, killing him instantly.

The security lights outside suddenly went out. And all the assistant could hear was her heartbeat, which was beating so loud and fast.

1c.

When the assistant managed to look squarely at the bed, she discovered that the occupant, who was supposed to be lying with a thermometer in her mouth, wasn't lying anymore. In fact, was nowhere to be found. She held her chest as though her heart was going to jump out her ribcage. While still standing bewildered, she saw a fox terrier run in through the entrance door. The fox terrier stopped halfway in and began to bark furiously. Sandra's hands fell loosely from her chest, and her whole body fell too. She fainted.

1d.

Sandra woke up on a hospital bed, amidst noise that is the medley of voices. At first, the faces she saw appeared as blurred images in her brain. She wiped her eyes and opened them gently. She immediately saw the image of the fox terrier and jumped out of the bed. Hands grabbed her, voices telling her she's in good hands. One of the nurse in the room made her sit gently on the bed.

"Where am I?" she asked, holding her head.

"You are in the hospital." another nurse answered. "You fainted at your workplace. Good Samaritans, who found you unconscious on the floor, rushed you to this place. You will be fine."

"What happened?" she asked, looking up and down. "What really happened?"

"We can't say exactly." the nurse sitting with her said. "We were relying on you for accurate information. Can you tell us?"

Sandra rubbed the edge of her left eye and said: "Everything's quite confusing. What about my boss?"

"He's in the morgue. What happened? What led to his death?"

Sandra heaved and shook her head: "The event that led to his death is still confusing and strange to me. There was this lady he suspected had Aspergilisantanus. I helped him place the lady on a bed after she fainted on his announcement. When she woke up, after hours of being unconscious, my boss and I went to her bed. My boss inserted a thermometer into her mouth. However, he had only turned for a minute before something bumped into him and killed him instantly. He just fell with force and died."

"What about the lady?" the third nurse in the room asked.

"She disappeared."

"What do you mean by she disappeared?" the nurse sitting next to her asked.

"I don't know what happened, but she was no longer lying on the bed. Still she was nowhere in the room." Tears began to roll down her eyes.

"Okay, now, I am on tenterhooks. Very strange." the standing nurse, whose name was Brenda, said. "Quite unbelievable!"

"Totally unbelievable!" the sitting nurse said. "Well, the police will soon be here. You will need to tell them everything you know. Okay?"

Sandra simply nodded and asked for a cup of water.

3a.

Contrary to what the Drugstore keeper thought, Gabriella was infected with a new virus that causes her to time-travel or teleport to another place with overwhelming speed and awareness - thus, this suddenly left her with a dual personality. Being a novelty experience she was yet to have control over, she mistakenly killed the Drugstore keeper and went back to Istanbul where she violated traffic rules and escaped from police custody. This time, she stole a parked motorcycle and rode into a busy road. She parked the motorcycle in front of a motel and went in to play a free game at the gaming centre of the motel. The hall of the gaming centre had televisions on its walls. She stepped in with her boots and latex clothes, looking irresistible and unbelievably alluring.

"Hola, chica bonita!" a man called out to her. "Come to papa. I'd like to buy you a cuppa!"

She wriggled her neck and smiled weirdly. She nodded and started walking up to the man who was wearing a sombrero.

"Hello." she said when she reached where the man was sitting. She posed, stretching her legs apart and putting one hand on her waist.

"Hello." the man said and stood with his sombrero in his hand. "My name is Vincente. What's yours, baby?"

"Funke."

"Funky?"

"Funke."

"Alright, baby. I'd like to buy you a cuppa and...and probably take you out to somewhere nice. What do you say?"

She shrugged with a smile. "Let's go somewhere nice, Vincente. Let's go now!"

"Let's go now, pumpkin! My love for you is an exotic dish. Let's go!" the man blurted out, overjoyed. Just as he was about to fasten his belt hurriedly, a picture of the lady he was about to leave with appeared in the news as a wanted criminal. The man's movement stilled like he was just electrocuted. He quickly shuddered and began to step back.

Funke smiled dryly. "But a promise is a promise, Vincente. We must go somewhere nice now. Please, let's go!"

"No! *Amare monstrum!* You are..."

But it was already too late for whatever. The young woman disappeared with great speed, smacking the man so hard it would take a miracle for him to regain his hearing, if he recovers at all.

3b.

Gabriella saw herself back in San Diego. She found herself close to a boutique and took the opportunity to disguise herself with the help of a worker and a mirror. She immediately decided to hurry home to her apartment. *What is this that has come over me?* She thought to herself. However, to get to her apartment she must go past *The Kepler's Inn*, an inn owned by a retired police officer. She quickly beat a hasty retreat, contemplating in the deepest of her mind what next to do. *Why fear when you've disguised yourself?* A part of her mind said. She turned again, without thinking much, and began to run to her apartment. She was going full throttle when the inn owner, who has been sitting outside, began to scream. The man began to pursue her down the street like she was Prometheus unbound.

"You are a criminal! You are a criminal, Gabriella!! You won't go scot-free!!!" the man kept shouting until she kicked something and fell.

4.

"The members of the jury now, with your claims, would want to know if who we have here is Funke or Gabriella. So, young woman, who are you?"

"My name is Gabriella Ifeka."

"We received information that you sent a communique to *The Flying Times* in Istanbul."

"That wasn't me. That was Funke Ifeka."

"Your twin, I must say."

"But, my lord, try not to make a mount out of a mole hole. I have objected to that idea. Funke is just my alter ego."

"Rubbish!" the judge shouted furiously. See, young woman, I don't believe in all those things you've been feeding my ears with. Stop talking as though a cuckoo made your brain its nest. This is real life, my dear - we are not starring in any make-believe movie. You'd better start clarifying me on the situation before I lose my temper and give you a relatively fair sentence! How do you explain your ability to commit crime in different places as identical persons in a slightly different time span?"

"I'm not the one committing all those crimes. It's Funke!"

"Funke my foot! If I hear anymore of that Funke, you..."

"But it's Funke, my lord!"

"Goodness gracious!" the judge exclaimed, fuming with rage. "Alright, so it's a Funke-assisted crime you've been committing. Fine. Fine! You...you are still guilty anyways."

"Objection, my lord!" the defendant's counsel said and stood on his feet. "I don't think she's actually guilty. There are such things as Time-travel and Teleportation."

"I have heard of such things." the judge said, nodding his head. "But they are all cock and bull stories to me."

"They shouldn't be to you." the defendant's counsel said.

"Please, no one should play with my intelligence. Does she have a time machine?"

"No, my lord." the defendant's counsel answered. "But..."

"You see? Ipso facto, who's fooling who?"

"But she's infected with a strange virus that allows her to do so."

"But that does not reflect current research. Anyways, who confirmed that?"

"Her doctor! Her doctor confirmed that there is a strange virus in her bloodstream."

"Hmm. Interesting piece of information anyways. Is the doctor here?"

"Yes, my lord."

"Alright! Let him step forward now."

The defendant's counsel turned and beckoned on the doctor who immediately began to walk towards the defendant's standing position.

"Are you the defendant's doctor?" the judge asked.

"Yes, my lord."

"Alright. What interesting piece of information do you have to give me? That this lady in the dock has a viral infection that enables her to time-travel or teleport?"

"That's correct, my lord."

"Hmm. I'd rather give my left hand than believe this fable."

"But that's the truth, my lord."

"It's no truth, doctor, unless you can prove it to me."

"But..."

"Can you?" the impatient judge interrupted.

"Well, let me talk to the defendant. But I warn that it would be a dangerous thing to demonstrate."

"Oh, perish the thought!" the judge said and chuckled. "We all want to see for ourselves, don't we?" He turned to look at members of the jury who all nodded in agreement. "Moreover, my astrophysicist friend thinks it's impossible too. Please, we can't wait any longer."

"Alright." the doctor said and went to have a word with Gabriella. And when he turned to return, the judge began to say something.

"And, also, I'd like her to go to Istanbul again. She's a wanted criminal there, so it would be easy to prove things."

"But she could be killed." the doctor protested.

"Alright! Anywhere, just anywhere. Let her just do her thing. We are waiting."

"But I warn about the consequences." the doctor said calmly.

"That the virus may be transmitted?"

"Not really. Not really, my lord."

"Alright! Enough of the talk. What I want now is action. Young woman, we can't wait!"

She stepped out of the dock gently and signaled to the doctor, telling him to leave. Of course, everyone was watching with rapt attention. The doctor obeyed and went to stand at the back of the court. Some people in attendance quickly obeyed their instincts and began to move back too. But no, the judge and the jury were bent on being right with their judgement. Some held their jaws with their two hands, others crossed their arms upon their chests.

Five minutes, ten minutes, fifteen minutes and nothing happened yet. Fuming with fury, the judge ordered her to go back to the dock.

"Miss, we are not here for child's play nor do we have time for any red herring. Now, please, go back to the dock. We don't have time for this caricature of self. I have to give my judgement and it's really pissing me off that..."

But the judge, somewhat satisfactorily, was interrupted with a flash.

5.

New York, USA.

"Challenges will always come, but challenges are also meant to be surmounted. Whatever happened to me must have happened for a reason. I wish everyone could time-travel to his or her future once in a while to see what kind of danger

our disappointments swallow for us. Who would ever believe that our office in San Diego would be attacked hours after I left because of my stomach problems? The lady who took my seat was shot point-blank. And she or I would have been dead months ago if there was bullet in the magazine. Anyways, thank God she survived the attack - even though she is still battling to recover from a kind of shell-shock resulting from the fact that a stun grenade was thrown at her. Sometimes, I believe, our guardian angels are fighting our battles for the overall good of our fate. But we know nothing about that, because we can't see the future. I doubt if I can be able to narrate this rollercoaster of an experience in clear language to anyone. Some will think I am lying with the truth. Yes, those who know me as a fiction writer would think there's some fictional embellishment. Anyways, it's my story and I must tell it the best way I can. Now thank you, Funke. You look so adorable on this paper's front page. Thank you for saving my life, technically. But you shouldn't have broken the judge's jaw - he was only doing his job. If only I can alter some timelines right now. But thank you for everything, for even the astral travel. Unfortunately, I don't want you back in my life - even though it has been a wonderful extraordinary experience so far. I want to be myself. Alright, sweetheart, goodbye now and forever. And...oh! I hope I remember to buy shampoo for my hair later."

She picked the syringe on the bed and injected herself with the miracle anti-timetravel-teleportation serum she produced with the help of her doctor, interjected, and went into a deep sleep.

CHAPTER TEN:

LIGHTS OUT IN THE CITY THAT NEVER SLEEPS

Find me a place in the capsule and watch me outdo Michael Jackson's moonwalk to the music of the spheres.
~ Wole Soyinka

Walkie Talkie Voicemail: "Evacuate the area, we think Murffins are lurking around. Spotted one. Copy? Evacuate the area..."

Tony removed his facecap and scratched his head. He had been exercising in the gymnasium of patience. It was getting dark, and he was yet to make contact with the Murffins - this fact bothered him like the buzz of innumerable bumblebees. He stood akimbo and allowed his mind to make a circination two hundred and seventy degrees on the pie chart of possibilities - the remaining ninety degrees, to him, seemed phantasmagorical like a dream. He tried to smile, but the effect was like pouring a jug of ink into a clear blue sea. He put his hand into his pocket and produced a handkerchief. He wiped the sweat on his face and turned to where the road bifurcated to the left and headed homeward.

***

It was now dark; and the street lamps stood tall and confident, staring down with luminous eyes like neon-eyed demigods. Mowlawn City was known for its technological advancement and its love of life. Everywhere in the city breathed with beauty and fun

- the nightclubs, the all-night restaurants, the Ferris wheel, the capsule hotels built from the Japanese prototype, the subways, the electric cars, the transcars (cars that can transform into different shapes), the wire transportation (this involves airconditioned cars for one person that runs on thick wires above the earth), the first-rate robotics, etc. Mowlawn City was the only African city that could compete favourably with any developed city in the world. Coupled with its economy and political reforms, it was no wonder why it made its country the first African country to become part of the First World. But, as the scientists would later confirm, every attainment of a new level attracts a new devil. Since what seemed like an overnight success, certain creatures have been attacking the city. Most times they creep into airplanes and try to hijack them. These beings were mostly metallic beings with green body fluids. They were not UFOs, of course. Scientists, gradually, began to identify them as the Murffins. These shapeshifting creatures were particularly noted for their ability to take the form of children when they want to be mischievous plus their proclivity for sucking electricity. Since their emergence into national consciousness, there have been dispatches tailored towards eliminating them or curbing their menace. But the more the government laboured, the more these creatures multiplied their numbers and their menace. One Professor Luke had claimed he had killed a number of Murffins while the stars were falling into his hands in a dream, and since then he has been shooting for the stars, maybe figuratively as well as literally. As an Astronomer, he would often say to his students: "If you are not shooting for the stars, you'd better not be shooting at all. Time's too precious to be wasted." And since then, him and his students have been planning on how to conquer some constellation and probably knock out some knucklehead Murffins.

But it had been, for the most part, a dream hanging on a thin strand of reality. One conspiracy theory had it that meteorites are Murffins who were dead for long, and that they needed a certain duration of time to become alive and live for another cycle on Earth. And so the conclusion for all of the conspiracy theorists in this camp was that Murffins were "meteorites" that were lucky to come alive on Earth. Many stories, however, did abound. Some civilians who could not stomach the outrageousness of everything were already losing their minds, no thanks to the police who made everything procedural. Soon, a children's television programme titled *"Who's Afraid of the Big Bad Wolf (or is it the Big Bad Murffins?)"* began to air. Children and students in general were being extensively educated about the Murffins to the point that a subject was created for it in all educational curricula. Mowlawn City became the target of local and international media - and, of course, that of every living conspiracy theorist. But the more media attention revolved round Mowlawn, the more many companies and organisations went to hell in a handbasket - but then, of course, what's death-ground for a rat is play-ground for the frog. So a few companies and organisations fared even better with the state of things. In a bid to eliminate the Murffins or curtail their menace, an organisation known simply as ET began to recruit and train persons who will help eliminate these Murffins and their menace. These individuals were called ET-P agents (and in some controversial cases, ET-P spies). These agents or spies sometimes wore tops with the inscription, "Murffins, why Mowlawn?" Simply put, their work was to make contact with Murffins. Freddy, the easygoing son of a billionaire scientist and investor, was the one funding the project. The man at the helm of affairs was Tony, a young man with intellectual vigour and a never-say-never spirit. A man who, sure, knew how to make lemonade from lemons thrown at him.

***

The candles of the night sky were beginning to fall asleep when Mmesoma woke up and parted the curtains of her bedroom window, a bedroom with some touch of the Jacobean. She had been crying last night and didn't know when sleep wrapped her up in its cosy blanket. Amen to that, or she would have had black rims round her eyes and a headache. Nevertheless, she still looked like gold dust on ice cubes. She sat up, turned on her bedside lamp, and peered through the window overlooking a lush garden. She could hear the dawn chorus of birds and the croaking of frogs, and even the chirping of crickets supposedly nearby. She wiped her eyes with her palm and checked the time. It was Five a.m. God knows she wished it weren't morning yet. How she wished not to wake to face her ugly reality again! But then she was awake, and the reality was still what it was. She yawned, stretched herself, and fell backwards onto the bed and closed her eyes.

***

It was morning and Tony was driving around, stopping briefly at intervals to observe a thing or two. It is certain there are people who act before thinking, and Tony had sworn never to be one of them. He was with another ET-P agent, whom he disliked at first - because when they first met, his pride sat on the peak of Kilimanjaro and he wondered if it has colleagues on Everest. They were yet to make contact with a Murffin. His partner opened a bottle of whisky and spat out through the window. He took a sip and handed the bottle to the driving Tony: "Care for some? It's Johnnie Goodyear."

"No. Thanks!" Tony said and checked his wristwatch. "It's too early for that."

"Okay," his partner said and took another sip before dropping the bottle. "Where are these crazy Murffins hiding? Do we need to storm the Galaxy with some Medusa head to find them?"

Tony looked at the side mirror and swerved into the street by the left. "They will soon be running out. They can't hide forever."

"But how soon?"

"That's what I can't tell you." Tony said and rubbed his moustache. "We are going to take a look at Ikenga's Fountain and Waterfalls."

"Why there?" his partner asked.

"I read some article that behoves my looking there. Don't want to be there?"

"No, that's not it! I'm going with you, are we not partners?"

"Okay. All way leads to Ikenga's."

As they got close to Ikenga's Fountain and Waterfalls, Tony stopped to drop some of his stuff with Brenda's Consignment Store. Not letting go of them, to him, seemed like window-shopping in paradise. He stepped out the store hurrying towards the car in which his partner was waiting.

"How's Brenda's?" his partner asked as he stepped into the car.

"I heard they will soon be out of business, a foreclosure I think."

"That's some badly-cooked rumour." Tony said and revved up the engine. "Brenda's dad owns a fortune. They are going nowhere."

"Rumours!" his partner exclaimed softly.

"It is what it is."

They had just parked outside the gate leading into Ikenga's Fountain and Waterfalls when they noticed two legs stretched carelessly out of the hedge by the road. They were human legs, no doubt. They walked carefully to the hedge, holding out their licensed guns.

"Go over there, see if there is a head." Tony instructed.

His partner went to look. "Sure. It's a little girl. Can I lift her?"

"Um...well, be careful."

His partner lifted the girl and came out from the other side of the hedge. "Her body's hot."

"We need to drive her to a hospital. Get the steering! I'll have the girl."

He took the girl and his partner opened the back door for him. "Give me the keys."

"Key's in the ignition."

***

Mmesoma woke up at about eight-fifteen a.m. She rubbed her eyes with her fingers and sat on the bed. She looked around and saw the picture she fell asleep with - the picture of the little angel she left as she fled from her madam and captives. A pushcart of foul memories overturned in her mind - and the oranges, the watermelons, the cucumbers and peppers were scattering and settling on the floor of her mind. Her mind was heavy. She was among those drafted to be sent abroad for high-class prostitution. The fleeing was not preplanned, and so she fled without her little daughter. It has never been her wish to abandon the little girl. She knew she loved her so much. Losing her now was akin to losing her happiness. She wished she could find her, even if it meant a part of her dying in the process. She was willing to put in whatever effort needed. She stepped down from the bed and went to brush her teeth, teary-eyed.

***

When they reached the hospital, they handed the girl to two nurses. One of which came to the waiting room and handed Tony a note. *It was found in the pocket of her gown*, the woman had told him. *See what you can make out of it.* Tony unfolded the note and began to read:

"It's a nightmare, I tell you, nothing much. I beheld:
Specs of dust blown about by the wind
Begin to settle upon rubbles, machines and flesh.
The boots eager to march march not.
Everything has come to a fullstop.
The world is silent.
War machines are sparking by themselves,
Looking useless from having nothing to destroy.
The machines humans created without foreseeing
A scenario where it would be Creature vs Creator.
Everything upon the Earth is a waste[1],
Tongues of fire wagging where the land is greener still.
A lot obliterated, except for a few things
Leaving what should stand as a proof
That there was once a civilization.
And can unending length of destruction
Wake a sleeping Euclid?
Survivors, impetuous and happy-go-lucky,

Rise and go for signs
That could point to a city or the totem of a people;
Some doubting if Atlantis ever was.
Years pass, and there are only anthills of a star world.
From every foreseeable sign,
You can tell that the survivors
Will start another war, the rise of powerful machines[2].
Is some clockwork of existence
Attuned to the music of recklessness?
Bleary-eyed engineers claiming indefatigable like Ulysses -
Some, later, standing with muting dust over them like Ozymandias.
A staggering new generation of engineers may come to the rescue,
Like Mike "the Headless Chicken" staging a comeback.
And can Laurel leaves enliven one's numbered days?
Just like a man with an uncontrollable zipper
Returns home to find more kids calling him daddy,
So shall they hasten unto their doom.
So shall they[3] hasten unto their unlucky end [4]."

He took a deep breath and passed the note to his partner:

"Naeto, take a look."

His partner took the note from him and began to read. When he was done reading, he folded the note and opened his mouth to speak but was interrupted by the doctor in charge.

"She's awake. You two may want to see her."

"Sure!" both ET-P agents echoed and stood on their feet.

"Alright. Follow me."

And they followed.

When they entered the room, they found the girl sitting on the bed. Tony removed his facecap and sat close to the girl.

"What is your name?" he asked, holding the little girl's hand.
She blinked her eyes and answered: "Tatiana. Little Tatiana."
"Where do you live?"
"Nowhere in particular, for now. I'm a street kid born to a prostitute."
"Where is your mother?"
"Don't know. Been missing."
"Siblings?"
"None. Please, can I be quiet?"

The men looked at each other. After a brief exchange of glances, they nodded their heads and granted her request. The doctor, afterwards, walked out leaving her with the two men. Naeto tried to produce the note from his pocket, but Tony signaled to him that the time wasn't right.

***

The early night of the next day, when they took her for a walk, they observed some interesting things about her. She was often making calculations with her fingers or stopping to listen to her heartbeat with a palm or just walking and saying something about a fountain. Or saying, *"I caught a butterfly in a blue spiderweb. Mamma mia!"* At first, everyone thought she was a mad little girl until a multitude of creatures appeared from nowhere and started charging towards them from a distance, each gradually changing into a kid. Elsewhere, on the busy road across, people were running and colliding into each other - cars piling up in the heat of collision. The Tower of the Singing Clock was clearly surrounded by different creatures, onlookers afraid their colourful tourist attraction may be razed. The glowing, colourful Tower began to fade in luminous glory as Murffins sucked its power supply. There was chaos, magnificent chaos. Just as the multitude of strange children were at close range (Tony, Naeto and the nurse panic-stricken), Tatiana closed her eyes and stretched her arms forward. Just then, Tony and Naeto realised the multitude were too close for comfort and woke from whatever trance or spell that left them simply watching. As they pulled their triggers to fire at the Murffins-turned-children, the lights of the city died out.

***

It was now clear that the city has fallen to a hungry attack. The city, however, was not silent. There were screams and cries and flashlights from colliding vehicles rising from every corner. Tony could hear a heartbeat from the ground where he was lying. He, however, wondered if he was alive or has simply drifted into a ghost realm. He managed to move a hand. It felt heavy. He managed to open his eyes - they quickly drank in the flashlights from a distance. He tried to make sense of his present state and environment. Suddenly, his olfactory sense awakened - he smelled blood and discovered blood was dripping from his nostrils. He tried to touch his nose with his hand, but lifting a hand seemed awkward and unnatural to him - more like an act he needed to learn. It seemed, to him, his hand and shoulder joint were a tile and a wall joined together by grout - he feared his arm may come undone if he applied too much effort. He tried anyways. And just when his hand found his nose, he felt a twitch in his brain. He could hear a voice, his auditory sense having picked up from where it left off - but it's more of white noise than voice to him. *T-r-r-r-r-*

o-o-o-l-l-e-y! T-o-t-o-t-o-l-l-e-y!! A-r-r-r-e...t-h-r-e-e? He tried to stand, but his body felt heavy and otherworldly. He, suddenly, heard clearly. "To...Tony." He felt there was something about the voice. The voice began to spread out in his brain, trying to become familiar. "Tony! Are you there?"

"Naeto." He has recognised the voice. "Naeto."

"Yes. Where are you? Where is the nurse and Tatiana?"

"Nurse and Tatiana. What happened, Naeto?"

"The Murffins attacked."

His eyes blinked reflectively in the dark - he has just remembered. "Are you sure we are alive, Naeto?"

"We are, my friend. We are breathing, I don't think ghosts do."

"But how come we are alive? You mean to say we survived an onslaught from a multitude of Murffins?"

"I don't know how we managed to be, but we did."

"You should have a torch with you. Or have you lost it?"

"Oh!" He began to touch his waist where the torch was attached. "How lucky! I have the torch."

"Shine the light."

The light flickered across Tony's face. Naeto immediately gave the torch another focus. "Where is Tatiana and the nurse?"

Tony groaned in pain as he tried to stand. "Did the Murffins take them? I mean, where on God's Earth are they?"

"I don't know. But we must find them." He directed his torch to focus at a distance. There were heaps of charred cars.

"Naeto." Tony called out in pain. "Come give me a hand."

***

DAYBREAK. TIME: SEVEN-FORTY FIVE A.M.

122

They were having a roundtable discussion-cum-breakfast - Tony, Naeto, Tatiana, Nurse Chikordi and Dr. Steve.

Tatiana, dropping the table napkin: "I just killed them all."

"I still don't understand." Tony said. "You mean you killed the Murffins with bare hands?"

"You wish I were lying." she replied and drank her juice.

"Not exactly. But it baffles me anyway." Tony replied, glancing at the others.

"Well, it's the truth. I discovered I am immune to them when they attacked me and my friends. They injured Ada before taking her and Helen away. I was left untouched. In fact, they started running when they got close to me and a part of their bodies began to disintegrate."

"You, I conclude, must be a special girl. I will take you to my lab. By the way, how old are you?" Dr. Steve said.

"Ten."

"Naeto, show her the note." Tony instructed, wiping his mouth.

"By the way," continued Dr. Steve. "How did you kill them all?"

"As they ran close to grab me or to just breeze past me, their bodies began to fall apart. I just had to make sure they died indeed."

"How did you manage to do that? I mean, the lights were out."

"Well, I have night vision."

"Tapetum lucidum. Interesting. All way leads to my lab." Dr. Steve said and looked up. "It's beginning to drizzle."

"Yes." Tatiana replied childishly and unfolded the note. "Oh, this? You took it from my pocket, didn't you?"

"I did." Nurse Chikordi replied. "Who wrote it?"

"A Murffin. When they transform, they call him the Speculator. I took the note after I killed him. I think I passed out after killing him - he was the hundredth Murffin I killed in the killing spree. I don't know if anyone should take this serious. Think it's best we destroy it."

"No, no!" shouted Tony. "We will keep it. Give it to me." Tatiana obeyed.

Nurse Chikordi flipped to the next page of the newspaper she has been perusing and saw what made her sigh. The caption read: *"Murdering Sunday: Murffins Kill Hundreds in Night Attack"*. She closed the paper and smiled at Tatiana. "Shouldn't we be grateful to you?"

The little girl smiled. "Be grateful to God, please. Somehow, I did it because I wanted to make mama proud."

And while still having their alfresco meal, they saw a group of three little girls in their finery holding umbrellas and giggling. Tatiana heaved a deep breath and enthused:

"They will soon be back. We must prepare for a seemingly last testament to a race war; this Earth's ours to protect."

"We must leave now." said Dr. Steve. They all stood up and set about to leave, Tatiana clutching the hand of Tony as they walked down the busy road of Sixth Avenue.

CHAPTER ELEVEN:

OXYGEN

Many men go fishing all [of] their lives without knowing
That it is not fish they are after.
~ Henry David Thoreau

Let's say it's the 60s. Pretend to be Bruce Lee or a future version of yourself. But Bruce Lee especially. You are in college, where you often skip classes to pursue a side attraction or "your passion" as you would love to call it. Pretend not to care that your skiving is affecting your grades. Pretend not to care at all. Because to care is to appear skittish, right? You and I know that "skittish" is not an adjective you would love to qualify you. *It's a man's world*, you often hear people say. You don't believe it one bit. *People should learn not to force their beliefs upon others*, you often tell your friends and your tight Gs. *All it takes is a strong widespread for one's beliefs to become something close to a diktat.* To your friends, you seem to have a good head across your shoulders. And the bottles, often than not, are always on you. You are life for the party. You are just classy to your fingertips; doesn't it seem obvious already? You work hard, you know it. You intend to join the army when you leave school; you intend to join with graduate qualification. You think you have the stamina and all it entails to join the military. Often than not, during your extracurricular training, you think you can throw more punches than Bruce Lee; your friends, at least, believe you can. The only thing missing in your life is rest; and if your life were to be a sentence, you need someone to put a caret in order to give you what you are missing. But you seem not to need it. You love your side attraction which is boxing. So on the weekends and some select days of the week, you make out time to do your boxing thing. Haruna, your college friend, follows you to cheer you up on the weekends; you love this guy! At least, he is the only one who sees potential in you after you. *Kai,* you love this guy! He is always there for you, from dawn to sundown. A rare fellow you think he is. You love him, but he has refused to introduce you to his younger sister whom you think is a little pretty devil - Hamzat, a conservative Muslim girl who you think has the prettiest face you have ever seen. You have learnt not to hold it against him. *There are many more fishes in the sea,* you think. You move on. You make a few more friends - more particularly female friends. Not like you are a womaniser, but you have roving eyes nonetheless. Amongst your newest friends is a girl who calls herself Jennifer Bullocks - You have never cared to ask if this is her birth name. You like her more than all your other female friends. You like her even with her rudeness and "lying game". Once, she told you her father works in the White House and said it was her uncle when you raised an eyebrow. Now when you check the number of women in your life, you can say you were wired to have hundreds by default. The tall, the short, the fat, the slim, and everyone in-between. But they are not your major problem. Your major problem is that you don't know why your grades are doing "a Jack and Jill". And you thank your stars that you have a loving Jennifer Bullocks to run to each time you need someone to talk to about your deteriorating academic performance. And of course, it ends well in the arms of Jennifer Bullocks; even though it does on a sheet that's not a result sheet. You begin to contemplate dropping out to face your boxing.

You visit your pastor to ask for advice, but you have a growing plan in your head. You decide to devote more time to boxing so you could become a boxing star at least. You, of course, go to practice with your loving J.B. Your friends and tight Gs think you two are a perfect match. You don't know if they are right or not. You often stride the streets of the city with her in your company. You think she's Godsent, but begin to believe strongly each time you win at the casino with her company. Deep within you, something says you should keep her for life. After all, you love money - but who doesn't? Just as you were having the time of your life, a rude awakening hit you from nowhere. A letter comes from your department, asking you to try another department or explore whatever options you may have. But it's not as if it's entirely your fault, the devil in his drunk episodes must have wreaked such havoc on you. You must put the blame on His Satanic Majesty - the man, everyone knows, is ruthless and deceptive. Damn him! You weigh your options and try to convince yourself that you still need J.B in the next chapter of your life. Now that life has dealt you a heavy blow, you must learn how to throw deadly punches during every boxing practice. You must learn the Mohammed Ali punch this time. You must put life to shame. You device a plan. You begin to work very hard for your boxing and military future. Soon, you start to have fixed matches where you roar like a lion, devouring your opponents. The money starts coming. But each time you knock down an opponent like a mannequin, J.B. demands you help her own a piece of clothing on a mannequin in any boutique. She's your J.B., everyone knows. And you must treat her like your own! You buy, you buy, you buy. Often suffocating yourself in the process. But then, you believe love comes with great sacrifice. After all, God so loved the world that He gave his only begotten son. You swear never to complain. You hurry straight off to uptown, you buy a condominium. You are happy the condominium is close to an essential emporium. You move in with no other person but J.B. *In a couple of years I should be rich enough to buy a mansion*, you believe. You keep boxing while also aiming for a spot in the military. You are at your A-game. You can throw good punches, your coach loves that. Lately, you have been on a winning streak. Your coach, too, plans to move to a new apartment - money is good. He has already started calling you "Money-making Machine". These days, you wake with the amazing body of J.B. next to you - Life is good! You think you should marry her, but the thought always crosses your mind in split-seconds. You believe no fisherman gets satisfied with one big catch when the sea is his to explore. So your boat you keep paddling. The side chicks are in numbers, they give you joy. Life is good. You forget your parents, almost. You return home only when the need arises - their sickness or whatever that necessitates your going back. You are almost a modern Don Juan. You are not a womaniser, it's just that you like women. You think you know what you are saying, even though you can't exactly tell the difference. Just like a deadly hurricane, a situation hits you badly. The Nigerian Civil War! Fear hits you down to your marrow. The root of the fear is that you fear being drafted into the Biafran army, that you fear going to war - a heavy irony. What were you thinking when you allowed the desire to join the army to creep into your heart? Didn't you know soldiers go to war? Or you only like the title and not the action involved? Maybe. You wake one morning and ask yourself what you are still doing in Nigeria. No one has asked you to fight for Biafra yet, but you can see it coming. You go for what should be your last boxing match. You win. During a private time with your coach, his friend begins to talk about a boxer who has joined the Biafran army. You can see what you dread about to come your way - he was persuaded after all. You get home in a fit of exasperation. You tell J.B. about your plan of running away. She listens to you with rapt attention. You want her to understand that two of you can run to "the promised land". She thinks for a while before she crouches to whisper into your ear: *Let's run, baby. Let's run!* You assure her everything would be fine, that you are taking her to a place where there is no war nor famine. A place where she can be safe for you, and you safe for her. *Let's run.* Five days later, you tell her it's Destination Canada. She gets overly excited and makes a quip. The people can go ahead and fight for all she cares. *Let's run, baby. Let's run!* You tell nobody, not even your parents - you think if you tell them they would want to come along. You don't have enough. You run, you and J.B. You run to Canada to start a new life. At least you will be safe from stray bullet or direct hit. You intend to continue your boxing career in Canada; where you'd probably show them that you are, no doubt, from the giant of Africa. You land in Canada with J.B. She grabs your neck excitedly and plants a kiss on your lips. You can see she's obviously happy. She says she will never regret the day she met you. You smile without thinking much about what she says. You tell her you two have reached "the promised land" where you two can live life to the fullest. She thanks you profusely, in a way you have never seen her do before. There is a remarkable glow on her face, a glow you have never seen before. She looks more beautiful than ever. Maybe you have been busy boxing away your life to notice how fleshy and beautiful she's getting. You smile, proud that she belongs to you. The idea of marriage hits your mind again. You allow it to linger a bit before telling yourself you need to have a sure foot in Canada first. You see a stain on her refulgent white gown and calls her attention to it. She screams in such a beautiful way that you couldn't help but ask her to allow you do the cleaning. You move closer to her only to begin kissing her passionately. Right now, you think you love her more than any one thing in the world. You two leave the airport and pay for a hotel room. From there, you two go to live in Yellowknife. The neighbourhood is conducive and quiet just the way you like your neighbourhood to be. Quite well, you are feeling nolstagic already. There is no place like home, right? You try to convince yourself you have everything you need to be happy in Canada - after all, you have amazing J.B. by your side. You gradually learn to lift off the tentacles of home, in the form of memories, trying to have strong hold on your soul. In the neighbourhood, you find it difficult to make friends. But when you finally makes one, it's a middle-aged man who's a grandfather of two. Unbeknownst to you, he knew two of you would eventually be friends. *I knew the moment I saw you that I could be of help to you*, he says. You barely paid attention to that. You just want to see how the friendship would fare. He tells you you can come visit him anytime. *Mi casa su casa.* You thank him genuinely. When the conversation suddenly becomes jejune, you tell him to excuse you and that you will most likely pay him a visit the following day. The following day, you are standing in front of his door with your fist raised for a knock. You hear a bark. You turn immediately to see him approaching with his dog. He is smiling and telling his dog that you are a new friend of his. The dog is still barking, but has just stopped now that it is sniffing your clothes. You shake hands with him and step aside so he can open his door. He opens the door. You step in with him to sit on his sofa. He walks out of the sitting room only to return with a bottle of drink. He gives it to you. You thank him and grab the bottle gently. He opens it for you. *Who's that wonderful woman living with you?* He asks. *Your sister?* You smile thoughtfully. How can J.B. be my sister? You shake your head. *She's my sweetheart,* you announce. *Wow! He exclaims. She's a goddess.* You laugh and thank him. *Are you planning to marry her?* He asks, sheer inquisitiveness in his eyes. You nod your head as an affirmative. *You should; her beauty is blinding.* But I hope you two are compatible. You shrug. We are getting along well. He smiles and let's the discussion digress. So you said there is war in your country, right? You nod, gulping down your drink. *Tell me more about it.* You relax and begin to explain the chapters of the war story to him. He is listening with great curiosity. You explain with great details, often demonstrating with your hands. You are still explaining. So passionately that you weren't paying much attention to the listener. You are still explaining when you hear someone say: *Who are the other girls I see you with when J.B. is not around?* With words still in your mouth, the question came with the effect of trying to choke you. You begin to cough, begging him to help you with a bottle of water. He goes to get you the bottle of water quickly. When he returns, you are still coughing with your hand on your chest. You take the bottle from him, uncaps it and begins to drink. Having taken enough, you heave a deep breath and begins to explain in excruciating details how you have been having a serious whooping cough. He tells you to visit a doctor. You tell him you have been visiting one already. You quickly stand, telling him you have to go so you can take your medication. He stands with a smile, shakes your hand and tells you to take it easy. You nod your head, rushing for the door. He follows you outside just to call out: *Hey! Don't start a war inside your house.* It could be worse than the one in your country! Your legs are feeling heavy right now. You stand for some seconds before willing those legs to take you home.

***

Days having turned into weeks and weeks into months, it's safe to say: How time flies! You are standing in your verandah, looking with arms crossed upon your chest. Not like you are looking at a particular thing consciously. You are just confused. Plain confused. Nobody, of course, can see the picture of damnation in your mind. You walk back into the almost empty house. You try to convince yourself you are just having a nightmare. But no, it's real. Now your bolts and nuts are almost coming undone, and you are looking for a spanner to fix things right. You run down to meet your friend. Luckily, he's at home at this time. You slump into the sofa, saying these words: *J.B., J.B., J.B....* Your friend is trying to know what the problem is. You are beating yourself up, lamenting about how all your labour is now in vain. Your friend is pressing hard to know. You let it out: *J.B. has left me! J.B. has ditched me! She left with all my money and property! I am finished!* Your friend is shocked. Are you serious, he asks as if you can decide to deliberately come acting. But you should know that's just a common question people often ask. *Dude, J.B. is gone*, you lament further. Have a deep breath, brother! Just say "All is well". You just can't hear him. Your sorrow is palpable. You are crying like the bereaved. He is trying to calm you down, but you think you can't be calmed. He is telling you so many things. Give it some time so we can really get to the root of the matter. Take it easy. A couple of hours is not enough to conclude that one's day is already bad. You are still lamenting. *Dude, I am finished! I am totally finished!* He stands. Let me get you a bottle of chilled drink. I'll be back. And just as he leaves, you stand and run out of his house onto the street and back to your house. It's clear some people don't know how to take pain or disappointment. It's true, and you likely know this. There, inside your almost empty house, you bring out a bottle of herbicide. You open the bottle of herbicide. You hold it tight and read your suicide note for the last time. You drink it in gulps. You smile and immediately go into indescribable death throes. You die.

And the story of your life suddenly ends with a few published chapters; the blank, unwritten pages ready to be lost in the antiquity of time.

You should have lived to put the last word in the denouement of your life story. You should have lived to see the twist at the end. You should have lived.

***

But excuse me, dear reader. Let's say you are Festus, the previously unmentioned protagonist of this mirroring narrative. What would you do with these wiles and woes?

You are grumbling and muttering to yourself, but I heard it all:

I will take whichever path leads me to a breath of fresh air, and try to find myself again.

Well, that was what I told Festus! And, just like truth is stranger than fiction, he didn't take my words. But the truth and the most saddening thing is that J.B. had wanted to surprise him by buying a better house with her savings. But it ended up being an expensive surprise. These days, when I remember his story, I say a quiet prayer for him. Sometimes I wish you too were trying to create a surprise as all we saw was the suicide note, blood stains and the bottle of herbicide; I hope you are alive somewhere. But months have passed now and I don't know what to believe. Peace wherever you are!

In Loving Memory,
Peter Drake Glenwood
(The fellow he met in Yellowknife).

CHAPTER TWELVE:

SONG OF SONGS

Nneka is not dead, but she wishes she was. What she has just seen is unbearable. What life is doing to her, she thinks, is not fair. She wants to die, but she won't. She wishes she wasn't callous.

***

Light rises on Chekwube, a young chubby girl with dishevelled hair and cheap worn-out clothes. She is going through her beautiful curlicues for the umpteenth time; she thinks her teacher would be impressed. The parlour, in whose centre she is, is a very furnished one. Her hands are on the glass-topped centre table, and her knees, in her kneeling position, bypass one foot of the centre table. There are numerous paintings on the wall - it's a nicely-built flat, clean, spacious, homely, inviting. A distant car horn seeps in, indicating that the house is situated at a commercial area, but not close to the main road. In no distant time, the sound of the horn is heard no more. The blinds of the parlour's only window, though wide enough, is pulled down and bright morning light flickers across the parlour. Unbeknownst to Chekwube, Madam Nneka had entered and is inflamed with fury. She walks away from the window and begins to approach Chekwube's position.

"Chekwube! Have you done the dishes?"

"No, madam!" she says, and runs towards the door leading from the parlour to the corridor before a knock overwhelms her. She sprawls on the floor, crying.

"So after I told you minutes ago about the dishes, you still had the effrontery to stay put, eh?" she kicks her, and her head meets the jamb of the door. "Stupid girl, stand up and go to the kitchen now!"

"Yes, madam!" she says, crying profusely.

Madam Nneka watches her as she walks quickly towards the kitchen. "Stupid girl! You think I brought you here for relaxation? You think I am your mother?" she sighs and flings her artwork to the ground. Today she finds no chance to say, *You swallowed a trumpet, see how you talk. Didn't your mama ever teach you manners? You go off to the streets and boom! You are talking loud and foolish. If you don't change, you will soon hit your death note.* She looks on for a while, and then makes for her bedroom.

Her bedroom is a work of art: there are paintings on the wall, a beautifully-designed chandelier, an expensive chest of drawers, a closet for shoes, a massive bed, and more things that an average woman cannot afford. This is her room, and she knows it! She brings out a diary from a drawer built into the wall, and sits with the padlock on her bed. She writes:

"Ever since my younger sister, Evelyn, married Eze, my life has never been the same. She took my happiness, my conscience and, eventually, my life. Why must she marry Eze? Or, why must she marry the one I love? These questions are two doors that lead to one room. The room of Jealousy! Yes, I have to be honest. Come on, what is it that Evelyn has that I do not. Okay, I know, this should have been in the past now, since I finally got married and have two children. But no, it is not! It is not, because Eze first met me. He would have proposed to me if Evelyn didn't stand in the way. And she happily got married to the love of my life! It is true they do not have money, and have brought their daughter to stay with me. I have accepted to help allay their troubles, but I loved

and still loves Eze. Oh Lord, I still love Eze! How do I free myself from this bondage? How?
Date: 27ᵗʰ May, 1999
Time: 2: 05 pm."

She closes the diary, and returns it to its drawer. She locks the drawer and leaves the room.

***

A fortnight ago.

"Darling, do you have some minutes to spare?" Madam Nneka asked her husband. "I want to discuss something with you."

"What is it?" her husband asked, dropping his favourite magazine.

"It is about our children, Kendrick and Monica."

"What about them?"

She sat close to him: "It is about their education. We've discussed this before; it is about finding them a new school."

"Oh, there you go again! I told you it was better if they remained in their present school. At least, for now."

"But…"

"But what?" he interrupted.

She hesitated, and then searched his eyes for permission to continue: "Um, those teachers, they are incompetent. Our children deserve more. Please, let's take them to Golden Group of Schools. That's where they belong! Please!"

He peered at her like she was gradually disappearing from his sight: "Please, let's discuss this again when we've tucked ourselves into bed."

She smiled: "Thanks, dear. Thank you."

***

It is the morning of 29th May, and the children are at home. They won't go to school because it is Democracy Day.

Kendrick, with a strained emphasis: "Mom, play Beethoven, Opus 57: Appassionata or Fur Elise. Appassionata or Fur Elise. Appassionata or…"

"Yes, mom I want Fur Elise. Play us Fur Elise!" Monica joins in, her face a fresh petal of a flower in bloom.

"Okay." Madam Nneka says. "That would be when you both are done with assignments. Okay?"

"Okay, mom!" both scream, and run for their schoolbags. The playing of classical music has been a routine in the house. A routine enforced by Madam Nneka. In her belief, it shapes the mind positively. And increases concentration! The home tradition has eaten deep into the bones of her children, so much that when they come back from school it must be classical music. Classical music before eating or classical music and eating; whichever way, there must be classical music. And how the kids love this tradition!

Madam Nneka, with a certain recollection: "Monica, please call Chekwube for me. Tell her to come swiftly."

"Yes, mom!" Monica answers, and goes right away.

She sits with her legs crossed, then falls into the sofa with her hands behind her head. She stares blankly.

One can hear the running steps of the approaching Chekwube from the parlour, as she comes from the corridor.

"Yes, madam!" Chekwube says, genuflecting. Her hands are covered with what looks like lather. She waits for her madam to say something.

"You are smelling!" Monica says, hitting Chekwube's buttocks. Madam Nneka half-laughs.

"Who taught you that, Moni?" she asks her seven-year old daughter. "Don't do that again, you hear me?"

Monica mumbles something incoherent.

"Um, Chekwube," begins Madam Nneka, "have you washed the children's clothes?"

"No, madam! I am still washing the plates. I just finished sweeping the house."

"Chekwube, what have you been doing since morning?" She looks around as though she is looking for something. Maybe something like the stiletto she once used on the girl's head. "Oh, I presume you are becoming sleeping Beauty in my house. Right?"

"No. No, madam!"

She sighs, probably because she can't find what she is looking for: "Maybe you want me to break your head. I think that is what you are asking for. When will you go to the market?"

Chekwube, impulsively: "As soon as I'm done with house chores."

"Will you get out of my sight? And, hey, don't forget to buy soy sauce from Mama Ejima's shop down the street!"

"Yes, madam!" Chekwube's voice echoes, as she hurries down the corridor.

"Stupid girl." Madam Nneka says, and turns to her children. "Have you both started doing your assignments?"

"Yes, mom!" they answer.

"Is there anyone who needs my help?"

"No, mom. My assignment is very simple," says Kendrick.

"Mine, too!" Monica exclaims.

"Okay. I will be right back." She stretches herself and leaves through the front door.

***

Two months ago.

Eze had come alone to say thank you to Nneka and her husband. Madam Nneka's husband was not at home. Nneka had expected this visit, but not today. Not impromptu. However, the odds were in her favour since her husband was not around.

"What do we owe this visit?" Nneka said, as she closes the door behind them.

Eze chuckled: "Am I not welcomed anymore?"

With a strained smile: "Who said that? Come on, I am your in-law. This, technically, is your house too. Please, have a seat."

"Thank you." Eze said, and slumped into the sofa. "How are your children?"

"They are fine. Probably sleeping or playing inside the house."

"Is your husband home?"

"No. Anything the matter?"

Not really." Eze began. "I came to say thanks to you guys for accepting to take care of our daughter, Chekwube"

"Oh, that? It's no problem." Nneka interrupted. "Let me get you *kola.*"

"No, don't worry. I won't stay long."

"I insist. I will be right back." She stood and went in. In about a minute, she came back with a bottle of wine and two cups.

"Ah, a bottle of wine! You worry a lot."

"It's no big deal." Nneka said, as she drops the cups into the tray on the centre-table. "Here, open the wine." Eze takes it.

"Remove your eyes o! I don't want to marry a second wife." Eze teased. Nneka laughs. The cap goes off. "Hold your cup." Nneka did, and he poured her a drink. He poured himself, too.

"Don't worry, if Chekwube comes, we will take good care of her. She's my niece."

"Yes. Thank you so much. Things haven't been easy for us since I lost my job. We can take care of her other three siblings. Thank you so much."

"It's nothing." She grinned. "It's nothing. Obviously nothing!" She grinned again; this time, longer.

"You have fine taste; this wine is really good."

"Of course. Of course, you know I do." Her gaze is now fixed on him. "Or have you forgotten that you and I have history?"

Wine spilled from his mouth, like he had just discovered a hidden flaw in it. He dropped the cup. "Please, Nneka, let the past remain in the past. I am married to your sister now."

Nneka, trying to defend herself: "So I am no longer attractive and woman enough, eh? Is that what I understand here? Eh, Eze?"

"That's an awful thing to say. Nneka, what I had for you wasn't love. I had a misconception. I am really sorry things turned out this way. I thought we've moved on."

She moved close to him: "Eze, I still love you. My love for you is still fresh. Still blossoming. I love you, Eze." She falls into his legs now.

"Nneka, please! Your husband won't take any version of our story if he sees us like this."

"The door is locked."

Eze found himself laughing: "You are funny. Look, I am married to Evelyn. I mean, do you want me to leave her for you, or to marry you both or to cheat on her with you? What?!"

"I don't know. You decide."

"You are insane." He picked his face-cap, and moved to the door. "Come and open this door."

"Please, Eze!"

He looked around and found the key hanging close to the door's jamb. He picked it and saw himself off in a huff.

Nneka picked herself up from the floor, and went to watch Eze from her window. She had expected something other than this. She had expected something wonderful, maybe a miracle. And she got disillusionment!

***

Madam Nneka, the housewife, has just returned from the market where she saw Eze. After several months. (The sight of the tall, dark, handsome man kindled something in her). She's home now, and with her diary.

"Why is this world not balanced? Why the unfairness? Why would a man leave a woman for her sister? What is love? Love is a song, and two should dance it. It isn't okay if one tangos alone; how possible, even, is it? How???

Date: 17th October, 1999

Time: 3:30pm."

She returns the diary, and leaves her room.

Someone is knocking, and so Madam Nneka goes to open the door.

"Good afternoon, madam." Chekwube greets.

"Yes. Thank God you are back. Please, drop your schoolbag and take food to my children; today is their extra-school-hours day. Please, hurry."

"Yes, madam!"

She closes the door, and sits to watch television.

***

Five years later.

The clouds are roaring. It is the rainy season and thunderstorm is paying its usual visits. The roads are wet and the gutters drunk with water. A loud thunderbolt comes and a gentleman almost dies from fear. He is, soon, holding his chest by the corner of a shop – Mallam Issa's kiosk. He beckons on him to come in. And he does.

"Please, Mallam, I am looking for 25 Lotus Street. Can you help me?"

"Yes. This is the end of Bewithus Street. Lotus begins from that junction." He points. "Just cross the road."

"Thank you so much, mallam."

"No wahala."

Chekwube's principal walks across the road, in search of 25 Lotus Street. In search of Chekwube. He is knocking on a gate.

"Who's that?" A voice asks.

"It's me."

"Don't you have a name?"

"I am looking for Chekwube. I am her principal."

"Okay. I am coming." The voice says, and footsteps move away from the gate. A minute later, footsteps approach the gate. "You can come in." the gateman says, showing his gap teeth.

"Thank you."

"Please, follow me." They walk a little before the gateman points him to an entrance where Madam Nneka had been waiting.

"Ah, principal! What a surprise! You are welcomed. Come in."

"Thank you, madam."

She leads him inside, and gives him a seat. "Is everything alright?"

"Yes. Sure. I came to see you," says the principal, before he recollects, "Aha, Chekwube wasn't in school today, why?"

"She has fever. We are taking care of her."

"Oh, sorry to hear that! I wish her a speedy recovery."

"It's alright. Thank you."

"Yeah." he says and brings out a paper from a file. "I don't have much time because I have to go back to school. Here's it. Chekwube has just received a scholarship to study abroad."

Madam Nneka, holding the paper: "Abroad?"

"Yes, I've always known that your daughter was destined for great things. In fact, I was the one who encouraged her to apply for the scholarship scheme. I am very happy for your family. Congratulations."

"My own Chekwube? Wow, this is good news!"

"Absolutely, madam! There's got to be a God up there."

"Yes," she says, nodding her head awkwardly. "Thank you principal for your efforts and care. I appreciate."

"It's nothing madam. I will be on my way now." He stands.

"Let me get you something, Sir."

"No, don't worry. And, please, tell Chekwube to get well in time for her mock exam tomorrow."

"Okay, I will. Good bye!"

"Good bye." The principal steps outside.

Madam Nneka feels a pain in her heart. She looks flabbergasted, shocked, almost unbelieving: "Phantasmagorical? Interesting. Chekwube? Phantasm! Evelyn's...? No." She wipes her eyes, an unholy thought rising like a tide in her mind.

Pause.

She paces about. She scratches her head. She nods vigorously. The thought still rankling with her, she leaves for her bedroom.

***

The following morning.
She takes the narrow path that leads to Baba Buro's Place, the herbalist shop.

"Good morning, Baba," she says, genuflecting.

"Yes, my daughter. You are welcomed to where solution lives. Welcome!"

"Thank you, Baba."

"Yes, what can Baba Buro do for you?"

"Um, I want you to give me a medicine for total sleeping."

"Total sleeping? What does that mean, my daughter?"

Madam Nneka, scratching her head: "I want medicine for death. A poison."

Baba Buro laughs. He laughs for long. Madam Nneka remains standing, uncertain of what to do.

"Madam! You have come to the right place. Come, sit here." he points her to a wooden stool. "How do you want to apply this poison?"

"Via food. Via food, Baba." she says, and then adds. "And I want a poison that takes up to three hours before working."

"I see." Baba Buro says, and raises a calabash from the floor. "Here, pick one." Madam Nneka picks. "Spray this evenly on the food of your to-be-victim, and you could expect a dead rat that day." Baba Buro laughs heartily.

"Just that?"

"Yes, woman! Pay your dues." He drops the calabash behind him. Madam Nneka puts her hand into her handbag.

"Here's it, baba."

"You are welcome! Go and achieve your goal."

Madam Nneka, stepping outside, breathes in heavily. She scratches her eyebrow and then heads for home.

***

Cut the onion, dice it into semi circles;
Be careless with it.
Cut the onion, but don't ask:
"Why must I lachrimate?"

"You said you'd be going to see your parents today, right?" Madam Nneka asks.

"Yes, madam."

"Okay. I will not be home early today, so I kept lunch for you in the kitchen. Also, there is a bottle of juice for you. Congratulations on your scholarship."

"Thank you, madam." Chekwube says, and heads for school.

Madam Nneka, with a sly smile on her face: "Poor girl! Who would ever suspect I poisoned her, when she was going to see her

146

parents. Their suspicion would be directed to indiscriminate eating of food with friends. Madam Nneka, you are bad!" she laughs, and goes in to get dressed.

Chekwube comes back from school filled with joy. She decides that she needs not the food, and concludes on taking it to her cousins. She dresses up neatly and goes to their school. She takes a taxi to Golden Group of Schools, and hands the food to Kendrick and Monica. (The school would dismiss in an hour, and the children cared less. The food they would have rushed home to eat was already in their hands!) Chekwube bids them goodbye, and goes to see her parents.

Left home
Not equal to Not returning.

"Daddy will buy me a toy today," says Monica, grinning from ear to ear. "Guess what it is going to be."

"I don't know, I can't guess." replies an uninterested Kendrick.

"A big teddy bear!" Monica announces, overjoyed.

Kendrick ignores the announcement, opens the door and lets her sister in. They are laughing, as they go in. Kendrick goes to the DVD player and summons the Classical music. Their classical music. Monica orders a change, and Kendrick effects it. They are nodding, they are falling, they are dozing. They are dying. They are …

Later, in the evening.

Madam Nneka has just returned, singing. With a sly smile spread all over her face, she turns the doorknob.

"Kendrick!" Her eyes has just seen something. "Monica! Kendrick, Monica!" She flings her bag to the floor, tears surging through her eyes. "Who did this? Somebody help! Somebody help!!" She wishes what she has just seen is a movie. But it is not. She throws herself on the floor, while the music continues to play. She lays still, until the last chord strikes, ending with a melodious note which falls cold. Death too is a song; at least, so she thinks and crawls weakly to switch off the DVD player.

***

And never, throughout that day, did she remember her diary.

CURTAIN

CHAPTER THIRTEEN:

THE BOY WHO FELL FROM THE SKY

Someone has been knocking on the door of Naomi like forever now, but nobody opened - at least, that was what it seemed to those who heard. Someone outside was knocking on the door of Naomi who had been indoors painting all day. Her bovver boots were left to lie almost alone, close to the door. The bovver boots were left to lie within the circumference of a blue hula hoop. Blue hula hoop that's quite new as the boots. Boots that were the colour of autumn leaves - a faint potpourri of colours you may call it. And amidst this beauty of belongings was someone seriously knocking. It was evening, if you must know. Quite well, neighbours heard the incessant knocks. But it is not quite often that the inhabitants of this neighbourhood are quick to react to what's not their business. Things were better swept under the carpet in this neighbourhood. And so, of course, their collective prompt reaction should elicit some kind of surprise in the mind of any of the inhabitants of this neighbourhood. People were trickling out towards Naomi's bijou house. They were going there in slow, careful, calculated steps. Actually, they cared more because they had contributed money for a project that should bring them household items for Christmas and New Year - and if you must know, Naomi was the treasurer! So, gently they went close to Naomi's house. When they reached and could not find anybody in front of Naomi's house, tired housewives which were in the majority folded their arms upon their chests and stared aptly. Their money was involved here - and if anything had to be taken lightly or swept under the carpet, God forbid that it should have anything to do with their monies. They watched with unparalleled inquisitiveness, which was never a thing to expect of these women battling with the minutiae of everyday life.

"Who has seen Naomi today?" someone asked, her voice shaky.

The women turned to look at each other, grave silence reigning supreme.

"I have been busy with knitting for most of the day." one said.

"I passed her house on my way to see a friend, and her door was locked." another said. "Maybe she's painting inside - we all know how she loves to paint, sometimes for the livelong day."

"But who was knocking?" another woman asked, a pertinent question.

A woman known as Madam T raised her hands and left her palms lying supine in the air. "I don't know o. Hmm, the last thing we want to hear is that our monies...is that our monies..."

"Have gone missing." a woman completed, seeing that the words were trying to choke Madam T.

"Oh, yes!" Madam T exclaimed. "We don't want to hear that."

"Could she be inside?" a woman wearing black scarf asked, and immediately added an incongruous question. "Doesn't she know what I can do to her if I lose my money?"

"Please, be quiet!" another woman said. "We need to be sure she's even safe. We need to find out if she's inside or not. Someone with her phone number should call her. We need to know if it was a robber hitting on her door or not."

"That's a good suggestion." Madam T said. "Is there anyone who came out with her phone here?" The women looked at each other, some opening empty hands to show they came out with nothing.

"Yes, I have my phone here!" a woman said from the back.

"Try her number, please!" someone shouted.

The woman with the phone began to call her. "It's switched off!" the woman announced, leaving the other women distressed.

"No, no. This doesn't sound like good news." a woman named Ruth said. "Let's try turning the door knob."

The women were hesitant to make a move. Then, Madam T braved the consequence and went to turn the knob. And, contrary to their expectations, the door opened!

***

As the door opened, Madam T quickly closed it and almost fell because she stumbled over the bovver boots. There was gasp of surprise from the women. Nobody had expected that the door would open. Madam T ran back to join the crowd.

"Is she inside?" a woman asked the dazed Madam T.

"I don't know." Madam T replied, panting. "I didn't really look."

"Hmm. We need to look." someone said. "Let me do that for all you frightened women."

The woman stepped out from their midst and walked towards the door. When she reached the door, she held the knob and called Naomi's name. "Are you there, Naomi? Is anybody at home?"

But there was no reply - none whatsoever. She gently turned the knob and let the door open slowly. Instinctively, she suddenly pushed the door wide open and stepped back.

And they saw clearly. All of them. And they saw indeed.

***

There in the expanse of room that served as a sitting room was the easel and the canvas Naomi loved to be with. Of course, the windows were closed - but the curtains were parted. Overall, the sitting room was illuminated - albeit with faint evening light. But now that the door was open, illumination was at the maximum. And the women peered from where they stood, each trying to have a clearer view of the room. Each trying to know if Naomi was standing by her painting paraphernalia. But, as they would realise, Naomi was not there. And when they had walked round the room and opened kitchen, bedroom and bathroom doors, they began to fear for Naomi's safety and...and...and their monies'. The women became highly panic-stricken.

"Has Naomi absconded with our monies?" the shortest of the women asked, tears coming down her cheeks. "Has Naomi?"

"No one can say for sure." somebody said. "We need to be sure she's even safe."

"Was she robbed?" another said with a sad tone.

"Heaven forbid!" an obese woman said, shaking her head furiously. "No, may it not be!"

And so the women continued talking and asking themselves questions until someone walked in through the entrance door and startled them. It was a boy with long hair, and he was carrying a red bucket of something. The women were startled to the point of being speechless, for never has Naomi been known to have visitors who stayed too long in her house. Since Naomi claims she has no relatives, seeing a boy walk into the house with Naomi not being at home should raise a cause for an alarm. And the boy himself, on seeing them, was gobsmacked. The bucket fell from his hand, and the liquid content splattered on the floor.

"Who are you people?" the boy managed to ask, his face serious.

"Where is Naomi?" a woman asked, as if that was an answer to the boy's question.

"Do you all know Naomi very well?" the boy asked.

"Yes!" most of the women answered.

The boy opened his mouth so innocently and broke the news to them: "Naomi had a fever and she's dead."

The news shook the women. "Where's her body!" somebody asked.

"Oh, it's out of town. She's dead and far far away. Dead indeed." the boy told them, going to the unfinished painting on the easel. "I am sorry for all your losses."

And at the sound of the last word, the women let out a loud cry. "You must take us to the dead body!" Madam T shouted. "That body owes us some money."

The boy smiled, putting finishing touches to the painting. "You see, I was with her when the dying occurred. Her death came, too, as a surprise to me." the boy started. "It was just yesterday that she started this painting on this easel, this painting that I must finish."

He coughed and sipped water from a glass cup. "You see, her death is quite a sad thing and yet leaves me with hope. She meant the whole world to me - even though she will no longer be here, she still means the whole world to me. She was quite humble, never caring much about the things that moves the world. She was such a beautiful soul. Nothing mattered much to her than her passion for the arts and her unquenchable pursuit for an admirably quiet and simple life. May her soul rest in peace. The lessons she taught me will forever be a guiding light to me, for it was her wish that I find my way and lead a happy existence. Oh, I can't believe she's gone forever!"

"But...but how did she die?" someone asked the boy still painting with his left hand.

"Oh, poor Madam Naomi!" he exclaimed softly and stopped painting. "She died while painting. This particular painting meant a lot to her. She wanted it to be titled *Grief and the Many Eyes of the World*. She really dedicated herself to it. I was her apprentice and she was my mentor and teacher. It's quite saddening that she slumped to her death while working early today. You see, Naomi has been sick for a long time. The drugs she became accustomed to left her with a medical condition known as Retrograde Amnesia. This means she only remembered things that happened after she developed the condition, while memories prior to the development are lost. As her condition worsened, she feared she might not be able to do the things she loved so dearly like painting and swirling the hula hoop - she was beginning to forget certain skills on an exponential basis. May her gentle soul find eternal rest."

"But...who are you to her?" someone asked.

"Oh!" the boy began and swiped his brush faintly on the canvas. "I have never known father nor mother. Naomi picked me from the roadside. I was wounded in the bush where I was living a savage life and had just escaped from a wild animal trying to kill me. That was eleven years ago. Naomi nursed me and gave me the little education I now have. It's quite understandable why she wouldn't let me live with her here. So I was living elsewhere with a woman to take care of me until she comes to visit. Oh, may her soul find eternal peace."

"Where is her body now?" Madam T asked.

"Sadly, it's in the mortuary. She..."

Just then, a man looking spick and span walked in and left the women more confused.

"Good day, everyone." he greeted with trained composure. "I am Doctor Wordsworth Odili. I am here to take him along for a brief interrogation at the hospital. Are you people friends of the deceased?"

Some of the women gave a slow nod.

"Let me hurry. I'll meet you outside soon." the boy said.

"Okay, I will be in my car." replied Doctor Wordsworth, and he turned and walked out of the door.

"I'm sorry. I have to go." the boy said to the quiet women.

They parted the boy, who claimed he was now the new occupant of the house, on the shoulder and nodded. At the end of it all - the narration, the gasping, the sympathy and the empathy - they realised they had lost the yearning to retrieve their monies.

And each turned, finding the way to her home.

CHAPTER FOURTEEN:

THE EXPERIMENTALIST

Abuja, Circa 3500

In a city in a country saddled with the task of meeting the technological needs of its inhabitants, rose a man with his invisibility. His name was Dr. Okoro. This discovery of his was a serendipity. Now, it will interest you to know what and what led to the discovery. And what and what he decided to do with it.

***

Dr. Okoro loved to play rock music, especially those with the sound of wah-wah guitar in them. He also had a thing for wind instruments, and owned a couple of them. He also owned a parrot and a cat. The name of his cat was Mushkin. There was no name for the parrot - poor fellow! Poor fellow who talked and talked and talked and still remained caged. Its master, ever since he brought it home, had never considered allowing it to flap its wings outside the cage. But despite the freedom that was denied it, the poor thing kept talking and talking - sometimes - to the discomfort of its master. His master who would have killed it on the day the thing couldn't just let him have his night sleep. He, eventually had to grab the thing from its fixed cage and put him in a carton, and took it into his toilet. And, sure, that was the only freedom the thing ever got! If that could be called freedom. Of course, Dr. Okoro was a no-nonsense man and had enormous love for his wife. The two lovebirds lived like two dovetailed pieces of wood - and it seemed nothing could ever separate them. At least, so it seemed. Now Dr.

Okoro was a Molecular Biologist who worked in a laboratory as a researcher. He also owned a clinic and seldom had plenty time for other things - except sitting under the cherry tree in front of his clinic to read a book or going for a walk with a friend or two. He was a dedicated scientist, so much that he was a member or a fellow of the Nigerian Society of Molecular Biologists (NSMB) and Molecular Science Society of London (MSSL). He was a dedicated scientist, he was a scientist par excellence. A man with great zeal for scientific inquiry. Everybody loved him even though he was famous for being standoffish. He kept a moustache and often wore white clothes. Often bespectacled. Often in his laboratory. Often in need of privacy which his wife won't let him get most nights. And on such occasions, he acted like a real gentleman and never complained.

***

"Oh, Peter Squire, spin me a yarn!" Dr. Okoro said and crossed his legs. He was sitting under his cherry tree.

"Doc, I'm being frank with you. That's exactly what happened. I am allergic to lies."

"Hmm. So you mean the man jumped to his death?"

"Yes. Because of his wife's tantrums."

"You don't say! Well, what has become of the woman?"

"Of course, she's alive. Eating the fattest calves from the farm and occupying space."

"Oh, poor bloke! He took his own life for the sake of his wife. It must not have been mere tantrums. You know, sometimes, the heart doesn't say everything. Well, may his soul find eternal rest."

Peter Squire removed his hat and genuflected; a sign of respect and last obeisance for his late comrade. When he was done, he stood upright and wore his hat again. "He will forever be missed. He was a lovely chap."

"Too bad he had to exit this way." Dr. Okoro said to Peter Squire, the VSO nurse from England. "Now, tell me: how often do you hear from the friends you left behind?"

"Oh, very often. Especially my wife."

"I said your friends not your wife. Don't I know how mad you are about your family?"

"But she's not just my wife; she's my bestie."

"Wow, I love that! At least you won't be jumping to your own death any time soon."

Peter Squire held his chest and laughed uncontrollably. "I won't even dare!"

The laughter became contagious and Dr. Okoro joined in.

***

Now, once upon a time, Dr. Okoro used to read only biographies and historical fiction. Now, while in his study, his eyes fell upon a title. *KING SARGAN*. He, when he was younger, treasured this book because it relied heavily on moral and how one man's tyranny left him and his country in cold waters of destruction. He remembered a page from the book and laughed loudly in between trying to lift the book off the shelf and trying to keep his glasses resting firmly on his nose. He took out the book quickly and hit it on his desk to remove the heavy dust that had come to be slathered on the book due to lack of use. He smiled and turned the pages intently. He reached a page and screamed excitedly. He sat down gently and perused the content of the page:

"Discretion is the better part of valour," men quote
When they reject a seemingly risky adventure.
But some are only expressing sour grapes,
With a treacherous heart latent 'neath a hallowed mien.
I doubt if any man is perfect
That live on this peccable sphere
Where all species are under an arcane spell.
Or did seemingly perfect Lucipher not fall?
Men, the scriptures affirm, are to dominate
Over the inhabitants of the globe:
Be they furred, feathered, skinned, scaled or leaved.
Yet, man still remains an ad infinitum slave
In the hands of Lust, Mortality and Dame Nature.
What serving-ruler men are!
Would it be despicable if I extol corruption pintly?
And would I be mean if I covet a man's sweetheart
Like God-loved righteous David did?
Or would I get a condign for defending a music
I think is sweetest, as Midas thought of Pan's
But received the ass's ears for injustice?
Or would I be a prey in a spider's web
If I try to circumvent the universal laws?
Of course, not! Who can challenge me?
After all, I am not Thor the Friend of Men.

King Sargan paused on the thought to sip his whisky. He rose from his chair, took out his favourite book, Twenty Famous Meanest Men, and walked languidly across the palace. He placed his pince-nez firmly on his retroussé nose. He was a tall and huge man with a pot belly. He was the king of his country, Green Coast; a country known for its criminal notoriety. His magnificent palace stood kilometers away from Green Coast's near-tumbledown buildings. King Sargan was one king, amongst others before him, that was highly feared. Nobody advised nor challenged him. Only the mention of his name posed a great trepidation to the citizens. He was a tyrant. Even his appointed chiefs were scared to tell him his wrongs; they were potential dead men. They, on most occasions, offered their wives to please their ruler. King Sargan simply got whatever he needed, by fair means or foul. His evil actions took place like a domino effect; one evil always led to another, and more.

Somebody knocked on the door and Dr. Okoro put his comb in-between the pages of the book and closed it. He stood up, adjusted his glasses, and asked who it was. What struck him first and most, if alarming, was the familial tone of the voice.

"Vincent?!" asked Dr. Okoro.

"Yes. It is me, brother."

Dr. Okoro wore his coat and went to open the door. Vincent was his cousin, a man with dreadlocks that often seemed unkempt. He smoothened his moustache and unlocked the door.

"Vincent! What an August visit! Boy, you sure don't look too good. How's everything?"

"Supposedly fine."

"Boy, don't speak in parables. Come, we need to talk in the sitting room." He stepped out of his study and locked the door.

"Vincent! Boy, how's your boat business?"

Vincent was about to reply when Dr. Okoro's wife appeared and began to tell her husband that breakfast was already served.

Together, they walked towards the dining room with Okoro's wife asking about Vincent's wife's pregnancy.

***

Au fond, Dr. Okoro was a perfectionist. A perfectionist with a lively mind that often channeled his existential energy to something creative and rewarding. He had a fecund mind. He had a Midas touch that could turn anything he touched into gold. He was extremely gifted. Jovial to a fault, but he also carried an aura of reserve about him. It was the rainy season and a Monday, and he stepped out of his car with an umbrella. He had parked close to his cherry tree, an exclusive parking space for him only. He closed the umbrella and handed it to Nurse Abigail who had come to greet him. And of course, he had stepped out of his car with Mushkin in the grip of his left arm. He rubbed the cat's head as he walked through the entrance door. Another nurse greeted him and he stopped, almost abruptly.

"Nurse Umbule, how are you?"

"Fine, sir!"

"How's your patient doing? I mean the child that has pile."

"He's getting well." Nurse Umbule replied.

"Good. Where is Mr. Jude?"

"He should be in the lab, sir."

"Okay. Thank you." He turned briskly and walked into a door by the left.

"Precious!"

"Good morning, sir!" Precious greeted on seeing him.

"Yes, if you don't mind, I'd like to see you and Mr. Jude in my office now."

"Okay, sir. I will fetch him right away."

"Good!" Dr. Okoro replied and left with his furry companion.

***

Saturday, six-fifteen p.m. Dr. Okoro wore his lab coat and sat across his lab bench. He had been sick three weeks before. Now feeling strong and healthy, he decided to go back to his rigorous lab experiments. But before he could lift a test tube, his eyes fell on an RVS strip and he decided to test himself. *It's just for the checking, I know*, he said to his interrogating mind. And he did not hear the independent part of his mind saying, *Oh, poor Igbo man!* He gently placed the strip on the lab bench, punctured his thumb with a lancet and dropped his blood onto the strip's end where there was the blood absorber. He added a drop of buffer afterwards and watched with ease. Of course his eyes was on the control unit of the strip. He watched with ease because he knew himself. He watched with ease because he expected to see only a line. And so when the result appeared, and he saw two pink lines, he slumped to the ground and fainted.

***

He wondered where she could be this night. Thursday night. There was no answer on the mobile phone. At the receiver's end. A man's heart was thumping really fast, threatening to jump out of its bony cage. He started feeling cold in his soul, so much cold that he crawled to the sofa in his sitting room. He stood up and lay on it quietly. Dr. Okoro knew himself, and to be HIV positive was a mystery to him. He had told his wife because he was a good husband, and because he wanted her to believe his innocence. He wanted her to stay with him in this particular trying time of his life. He needed her to understand that it was not his fault - and of course, his wife asked if it was hers. To that note she tested herself and the result came out negative. Dr. Okoro further pleaded and asked for time to figure out how he got the virus. His wife listened and promised to give him time to come up with an explanation for how he contracted the virus. But her absence this night...with a few of her belongings, as Dr. Okoro later found out, signified that she may never be coming back to stay. So Dr. Okoro lay on the sofa and wept for what he believed could never have been his fault.

***

Friday night. And as Dr. Okoro tried to sleep with his sorrow, he received an SMS from his wife which read: *I have moved on with my life, and I think you should do the same.* The message disturbed him so much that he did not sleep this night. Hands of depression held his throat and began to squeeze peace out of him. He, with a heavy heart, removed his pyjamas and slept with his boxer shorts. This very night, he shucked corn in his dream.

***

Monday night. If you are *au fait* with human psyche, you will know that challenges and depression can push one to greater heights, can push one to become better - this, of course, is if one decides to wear the cloak of positivity. So, still battling with his depression, Dr. Okoro went back to his abandoned project - the herculean task of finding a cure for HIV. Now that he was infected with the virus was the best time to give the project another try. So, with his wife gone AWOL, he spent most of his nights with test tubes, beakers, petri dishes and the likes. Sometimes, that is if his self-love bar rises, he spent his night with a pillow and a blanket. He often slept in his laboratory, him and Mushkin. This night, in his dream, he almost danced on banana peels.

***

Wednesday morning. It was raining, so Dr. Okoro wore a parka to his clinic. As the nurses greeted him, he wore a smile - the smile, which he knew too well, was a carapace that tried to hide the troubled innards of a man on the brink of collapsing or a thing worse than that. Even with the cold, he felt his body was burning. *To what do you owe this hyperpyrexia?* His mind asked. He knew the answer but, if he must stay collected, must parry the question. His peripheral vision revealed a nurse running towards him and shouting something, but he did not turn nor did he bother to stop. In the world he was living in now, to stay peaceful was to avoid human contact whenever he could. He turned the door knob of his lab door and locked himself inside. He had started to undergo what Mr. Jude would call "Induced Hibernation". And now, if you must mention that name near him get ready to absorb the impact of a flying mass with your head. Was it not Mr. Jude that made him to transition from HIV negative to HIV positive? He was so sure it was him.

Okay, you don't know, Dr. Okoro was a haemophiliac. Dr. Okoro had been sick before he tested himself, you know this. It was Mr. Jude that tested the blood that was transfused into him when he lost a lot of blood due to hemorrhage, Mr. Jude was his clinic's laboratory technician - you wish you knew all this, but you do now. And for the million dollar question, WHERE IS MR. JUDE THEN? Dr. Okoro had sacked him for gross sexual misconduct with patients and nurses. Did he even test the blood?

Inside his laboratory, Dr. Okoro's eyes crinkled behind his glasses. A green effervescence went up in a lovely curl, Mushkin jumped across the lab bench and landed on the floor with shards and liquids. Dr. Okoro screamed within five seconds of the incident and tried to gather himself in more than ten.

***

When, finally, he gathered himself he discovered Mushkin was no more. He began to fidget. He was perturbed, he was perplexed, he was flabbergasted, he was discombobulated, he was everything you could think of. Then, like a horror movie, he heard a new close to his leg and he shouted his own name by way of surprise. He was taken aback. He stroked his moustache, summoned courage, and squatted. He made a move that seemed like he was grabbing the air. And the move yielded Mushkin in his hands. Astounded, he let go. The cat made more mew sounds before Dr. Okoro bent down and grabbed the invisible cat.

***

Dr. Okoro, still not able to see his Mushkin, locked the thing up in a big airy box. He sat afterwards and ruminated: *What sort of chemical cornucopia must have led to the invisibility of Mushkin? I was mixing ethanol and...Whatchamacallit. Ah, no, Mushkin must have overturned other chemicals into my test container! Invisibility? No, I must get to the root of this.*

He stroked his moustache and proceeded to wear his gloves. He noticed a bluish chemical was dropping to the floor from his lab bench. He picked a rag and wiped his lab bench clean. He adjusted his glasses and decided to sweep his lab first. While he was outside trying to dispose the shards and dirt from his lab into a trash can, Nurse Abigail greeted him. He waved a hand at her and returned to his lab bench. It was already evening and he knew, perhaps, Nurse Abigail wanted to inform him that she would soon be on her night shift. *Oh, caring Nurse Abigail should just go! I will be fine,* he thought. Nurse Abigail had been acting like a wife to him ever since she knew about the fact that his wife left him. He had just picked up a pipette when somebody started banging on the door. He went to the door and looked through the peephole. It was Nurse Abigail! *Oh, not again!* He opened the door.

"Nurse Abigail, what is it?" he asked. "Is any patient looking for me? What is the work of Dr. John?"

"No, I was just checking on you."

"Oh, thanks. Quite thoughtful of you. Now, you see, I am fine."

"Okay, I will be going..."

"On shift." Dr. Okoro completed.

"Yes."

"Good. Now, hurry before the downpour gets too heavy seeing that you are wearing such good shoes. I was in the middle of something, do have a good night."

"Thank you, sir."

He quickly closed his door.

There was a feeling of something familiar hovering in his mind space, albeit vague. This very night, he slept with a real smile on his face. He had an actual sleep, his first since many days of being depressed and floating in-between consciousness and unconsciousness.

***

Thursday morning. He woke up and could not turn his neck with ease - he must have slept with his head not properly placed. He rubbed the back of his neck gently and tried to put away his pillow. He stepped out to brush his teeth and just then, for the first time since he started sleeping in his lab, it dawned on him that his employees may be gossiping about him with regards to his strange behaviours. Well, he pushed away the thought with ease and walked back into his lab. Door closed!

***

01:00 P.M. EAT

Dr. Okoro tumbled from his chair, reached the floor and shouted "Eureka!"

***

01:50 P.M. EAT

Dr. Okoro stepped out of his lab, locked the door with a visible cat in his left hand. Smiling uncontrollably, he walked away from the door of his lab.

    "Good morning, Sir!" Nurse Umbule greeted.

    "Yes, a very good morning to you."

"Good morning, sir!" Nurse Ngozi greeted.

"Yes, a very wonderful morning to the world."

"Good day, sir!" Nurse Abigail greeted.

"Oh, good day, Abigail. Isn't the day so good?" He suddenly halted, put his hand in his pocket, and said: "Abigail, take this money and give yourself a treat for the sake of a good day."

"Thank you, sir!"

"Oh, Abigail, don't thank me. Thank the day."

He continued replying to all greetings with great elation until he entered his car and drove off. And drove off to have a drink or two with a few trusted friends. At this very moment in his life, in his imagination, he was moonwalking.

***

18:00 P.M. EAT

Having known what led to the disappearance of Mushkin + having produced a "reappearing mixture", he returned to his lab to try the "disappearing mixture" on himself.

***

18:40 P.M. EAT

Dr. Okoro could not control his euphoria when he stepped out of the lab and walked past people without them seeing him. Excitement closer to madness almost choked him. He ran back to his lab to check if he could see himself with a mirror. And...

He was able to see himself. *So I can see myself but others can't see me?* He said to himself, feeling amazed.

He smiled at the reflection of himself in the mirror and sat down to make a list of things he must do with his invisibility the next day.

***

And the next day finally came. And Dr. Okoro stepped into the world with his invisibility. All the plans on his list bored down to one precise and, as it seemed to him, elegant motive: *Scare the shit out of people!*

***

To become invisible together with his clothes or hat or shoes, as he later found out, he must smear the chemical onto such piece of wear and allow the liquid to permeate onto his skin. If not, he would have to go naked. He abhorred the latter. So he dropped some of the liquid onto his shoes, smeared it on his clothes and went invisible.

And out on the streets and main roads was he, talking children away from the custody of their parents and getting enough entertainment as they contemplated between running for their lives and running after their floating children crying for help. And for everywhere he went, there was a type of confusion that was left behind. Sometimes, he introduced himself as Mr. Wind to his victims - most of whom fainted from shock and fear. And so gradually, with the commotion that had risen on the streets and main roads, policemen were all over the streets and main roads of Abuja trying to solve the puzzle - trying to solve what, arguably, should be the greatest puzzle of the 4th Millennium.

***

Days turned into weeks and weeks into months and no one could demystify the case of the invisible Mr. Wind. Ads with the caricature of him as a mass of strong air began to appear on billboards with captions like, "Help Yourself, Help Your City, Help Your County: Do You Know How We Can Capture Mr. Wind?" or "Capture Mr. Wind and Win Millions; Offer Valid While the Mystery Last". People began to live in terror as many victims who couldn't take the shock were often lying dead when found.

***

So when Dr. Okoro discovered that his actions were becoming life-threatening to his countrymen, he decided to stop playing pranks and instead put his invisibility to good use. And so one day, he drove to the woods on the outskirts of the city and walked into it to test his invisibility in new ways - ways that could be of benefit to mankind.

***

Sometimes things don't happen the way we suppose they should, and even gods, to their chagrin, can be astonished. Dr. Okoro had just gone invisible when he decided to climb a tree. But unknown to him, the branch he had decided to stand on was dry and naturally out of bounds for heavy weights. So he fell and landed with a sharp pointed object he brought along piercing his chest. Suddenly a lesson presented itself and he knew he will not live to share it: That *good intentions aren't enough when fate takes centre stage*. So, Dr. Okoro took a deep and final breath and died invisible. And this was how Dr. Okoro's disappearance and the identity of Mr. Wind became a mystery and a story that lived in the hearts of men.

CHAPTER FIFTEEN:

THE FLIGHT ATTENDANT

Maryann is a flight attendant. No, Maryann used to be. She just resigned two days ago - you may later ponder if "resign" should be the appropriate verb here. Let me take you first to the likes of Maryann. Maryann likes books; Maryann likes peppersoup, periwinkle and peppered snails. Maryann could be your sweet sister, that one that wants to make you happy all day. But no, Maryann will not tolerate your foibles if she holds you in high esteem. That's Maryann! Let's rewind to when Maryann was a flight attendant (and how she did become).

Maryann works for Kwin Airlines. Before landing this seemingly amazing job, she has been dealt heavy punches by life. She has watched her family suffer as a result of poverty. Maryann, like she used to say, can "teach you Hunger 401". She often says, "I am a professor in the course, don't ever argue with me." No one has ever wedged a successful argument against Maryann. So in a quest to find a better life, she applied for the limited position of a flight attendant at Kwin Airlines. How she got to know about the job opportunity is a miracle in itself. By stroke of chance, she slept her way into the job. Her luck came glittering when on a hot Sunday afternoon she overslept in the bus she boarded. By oversleeping, she passed her destination. By oversleeping, she had to be woken up by the conductor and driver of the bus. She woke up with a start and demanded to know what charm or juju they had used on her that made her to miss her destination. They had stopped her at a gas station and were in a hurry to get a refill.

"What did you two do to me?" she demands to know.

The bus conductor, fuming with impatience and anger, drew her out of the bus and she almost falls to the ground. "Wetin dey do this one? You dey suffer from sleeping sickness? Please, pay us our money!"

Maryann, still trying to maintain a centre of gravity: "Do you want to injure me?" How much is even the money?"

"One hundred and fifty naira," replies the impatient conductor.

"What?! Are you joking?!"

"Okay, when you were enjoying the ride you didn't know?"

"This is not where I was supposed to stop, I have to board another bus that will take me back."

"Tell that to the petrol we burnt. Please, pay us our money."

The driver pays for the refill he has just gotten and gets ready to enter his bus. "Oya, make we go."

"Oga, she never pay o!" the bus conductor tells him.

"Olorun!" exclaims the driver. "Please, passenger, what is your problem? Pay us, we don't have time to waste."

"Please, I can't pay one hundred and fifty naira. I can only pay eighty naira."

"No, it can't be eighty naira!" the driver corrects. "That should have been the fee but not anymore, not after you reached this place. Please pay us fast, you are wasting our time."

"I don't have a hundred and fifty naira, please collect eighty naira."

"What kind of witchcraft is this?!" barks the conductor. "Pay us make we leave here, which kin' nonsense be this?"

"But I don't have..."

"Hey, what's the problem?" a man on white tuxedo asks.

"Tell this girl with *puff puff* cheeks to pay us!" says the impatient bus conductor.

"My lady, what is the problem?" the man asks in a polite manner.

"I overslept in the bus and missed my destination. They want me to pay more than I can afford to pay. I can't give them a hundred and fifty naira, I know..."

"It's alright!" interrupted the gentleman. "Driver, here's two hundred naira. You can keep the change." He hands the driver the money.

The conductor collects the money quickly and tells the driver to start the bus.

"Thank you, sir!" Maryann says, genuflecting.

"It's nothing. Everyone gets into trouble once in a while. What is your name?"

"Maryann, sir!"

"Okay, where do you live? I can drop you off."

"Really?" Maryann asks, a luminous smile adorning her face.

"Yes. That's my car over there. Come!"

"Oh, thank you. That's quite kind of you. So there are still good people in this world?"

"I don't know if I am really good. Here, enter!" He holds the door open for Maryann.

"Of course, you are!"

"Okay then, thank you." He closes the door and goes for the driver's seat. "Where do you live?"

"I live at 60 Mangrove Street off Zinga Road."

"It's alright, I'll take you there."

"Thank you, sir."

"It's nothing." He starts the car and swerves into the road. "What kind of job does a beautiful girl like you do?"

"I am a sales girl. I work in a supermarket."

"Oh, that's good." he replies, looking at the rear-view mirror.

"Really?"

"Well, it is better than nothing."

"Okay, that sounds logical. I am sorry if it offends you, what is your name?"

"Seth." He swerves into the street by the left.

"Okay." Maryann replies, looking at him carefully.

"Mangrove Street is after this street, right?"

"Yes."

"Good. When we get to 60 Mangrove, please tell me."

"Okay, sir."

"And by the way, won't you like to work in an airport?"

"Airport? Ah, I will appreciate that."

"It's alright. Here's my card, call me whenever you are free."

"Thank you, sir!" Maryann replies as she collects the card from him. "Thank you for your immense kindness. God bless you."

"It's alright. We all need help sometimes."

"There, there! No. 60 Mangrove Street is by that corner."

"Okay. You are finally home, isn't it?" Mr. Seth asks, smiling.

"Yes, it is. Thank you so much, I have never experienced this sort of kindness. May God bless you."

"It's alright." Mr. Seth says and stops in front of a green gate. "My regards to your parents."

"Alright, and take care." Maryann says before stepping out of the car. "I'll call you."

"That's good. Till then." He makes a U-turn and Maryann waves him a goodbye.

***

Under a star-lit Tuesday night, and with the company of fireflies, Maryann proceeds to call the kind Mr. Seth. She sits under the mango tree in their compound and crosses her legs. By sitting under the mango tree, at the spot where she is, she finds herself facing their house's patio. On this patio sits her often absentminded grandfather. Her grandfather's face is revealed momentarily by a flicker of light from inside the house and just then, Mr. Seth picks her third call.

"Hello. Good evening, sir."

"Good evening. Who's on the line?"

"Oh, sir, it's me! It's Maryann!"

"Maryann?"

"Yes, Maryann from 60 Mangrove Street."

"60 Mangrove Street?"

"You dropped me off on Sunday, don't you remember?"

"60 Mangrove Street? I can't remem...oh, Maryann! How are you?"

"I am fine, sir!"

"I almost couldn't remember. How are you? How are your people?"

"Fine, sir! We are all fine, sir!"

"That's good. You called with regards to the airport job, right?"

"Yes, sir! Is it still available?"

Just then, the call gets disconnected. Embarrassed, Maryann looks at the screen of her phone. She sighs and curses: "This damn phone, this damn phone again. Always going off without being switched off. I really need to buy a new phone." She brings out the battery, taps it furiously and returns it to where it belongs. She switches the phone on again and proceeds to dial Mr. Seth's number again.

"Hello, sir! It is still Maryann. I am sorry about the first call being disconnected, my phone is faulty."

"Is alright, I don't want to waste your airtime. Meet me at the same gas station where we met. Call me by ten a.m. tomorrow, I'll come and pick you up. Make sure you dress nice and decent."

"Okay, sir! Thank you, sir! God bless you, sir!"

"It's nothing. Tomorrow then."

"Okay, sir. Thank you. Good night, sir."

"Alright, good night."

Maryann disconnects the call and gasps in excitement. "Thank you, Lord! Thank you, father!"

"What is it, Maryann?" her grandfather asks in a low-pitched tone.

"Nothing, papa." she replies and rubs the old man's shoulder. "Have you eaten your food?"

"Yes. Yes."

"Okay. Let me go inside for a while."

"Okay. Okay, just go."

Maryann dances as she goes in, peeking at the firefly cupped in her hand.

***

The next day. Maryann wears her blue bell-bottoms and white long-sleeve top and goes to meet Mr. Seth. She, of course, does not not forget to apply her perfume; and so she oozes with flamboyance and confidence as she leaves home for the gas station.

Mr. Seth had asked her to call him by ten a.m., and so she calls him while inside the bus. She calls him at exactly ten-fifteen a.m.

"Hello, sir! Good morning."

"Good morning. Maryann, how are you?"

"Fine, sir!"

"Okay."

"Sir, I am on my way now. I will wait for you at the gas station."

"It's alright."

"Okay, sir. Thank you."

"See you there."

At the end of the call, Maryann sits well and returns the phone to her handbag. She does a prayer marathon in her mind and wishes things would never go wrong, wishes for the odds to be in her favour. She induces herself into relaxation and tries to enjoy the ride. As she rides on, little beads of perspiration starts to surface on her forehead and nose. In her mind, she wonders what kind of job might be offered her at the airport. Now, the bus is getting closer to the gas station, she holds the artificial limpet attached to her necklace and closes her eyes. Maybe she prayed, maybe she imagined herself living a better life, maybe she did it on a whim. When she opens her eyes, the bus is already an inch closer to the gas station and she jumps up thinking she would have missed her destination again.

"I'll come down here!" she shouts, startling the people sitting close to her. "Please, please, stop the bus! I don't have any interest in going further."

The bus comes to a halt. She forces her way through the passengers, pays the bus conductor, and alights. She produces a handkerchief from her handbag and wipes her sweaty face. She looks around herself energetically and then allows her eyes to take quick looks at her dress and her shoes. She bends down and wipes away the dirt on her bell-bottoms and shoes. Afterwards, she stands up and makes her way into the premises of the gas station. She checks her wristwatch and the time is ten-twenty a.m. She walks towards the restaurant inside the premises with the intent of waiting for Mr. Seth there. She fastens the straps of her handbag firmly to her shoulder and sashays towards the restaurant. As she is walking towards the restaurant, a man standing by a car taps her on the hand and she turns sharply.

"Maryann?"

She looks at the person shocked and nervous. Beyond her expectation, it is Mr. Seth. She gasps with the mixed emotion of surprise and excitement.

"Mr. Seth! You are here already? You scared me." She holds her chest with two hands.

"I am sorry," Mr. Seth says, laughing mildly. "I didn't mean to. Come inside the car let's talk plus you need to rest due to the risen adrenaline."

Maryann heaves and heeds.

"I am sorry I scared you. Hope you will be okay." Mr. Seth says to her inside the car.

"Yes, I'll be fine."

"Okay. I am really sorry. Here, take some water." He hands her a bottle of water.

"Thank you." She collects the water.

"With respect to the job, my brother works as a pilot at the airport. He told me something like the airport recruiting new fight attendants. He also said the vacancy is limited. Are you interested?"

"Flight attendant? What is the work of a flight attendant?" Maryann asks.

"A flight attendant, often than not, is a young woman employed by an airline primarily to ensure the safety and comfort of passengers. A flight attendant should be a young woman who's not married, and ought to be beautiful. The marriage restriction thing has been relaxed though. You have what it takes to work for Kwin Airlines, don't you think so?"

"Wow! Such a privilege! I like the job. How do I apply?" Maryann asks with a smile.

"Splendid! I'll drive you to the airport so you can pick the form. Don't worry, I'll pay the ten thousand naira fee."

"Ten thousand?! Oh, thank you sir! Where would I have gotten such amount of money? Thank you, sir. May God bless you." She tries to hug him.

"Oh, please! There is no need for this. Everyone deserves a miracle once in a while. Let's hit the road right away." He keys into the ignition and the engine revs up. The car finds its acceleration and they set out for the airport.

***

As is the expectation of the Airline, Maryann fills and submits the form within forty-eight hours of receiving it. She, of course, expects to receive a favourable reply. She keeps calling Mr. Seth while waiting and expecting a reply. Then two weeks later, she picks up her phone to call Mr. Seth and sees an incoming call. She picks the call casually and, then, the miracle happens.

And that is how she went to work for Kwin Airlines.

This is how she became a flight attendant.

***

Now, Maryann works for Kwin Airlines. The uniform looks so nice on her that to behold her is to be blown away mentally. The Kwin Airlines flight attendant insignia glows conspicuously on her chest. The first flight she is to service will be heading to Australia, that's Flight 474. Her months-long training means she can handle any emergency situation that may arise inside an airplane. Impulsiveness tells her to do this: stand by the fuselage of the airplane and take a quick selfie! And she heeds. Yeah, having a selfie on your first day at work will certainly do no harm. Will certainly do no harm if you also do not have the intention of finding yourself, by whatever means, sitting by the propeller. She climbs, afterwards, to inspect the airplane with other members of the cabin crew. They check the seats. They check that the number of life vests are adequate. They check the cockpit. They check everything that needs to be checked. Everything is in good shape, and this means they and the pilot can fly the passengers to their destination. Australia.

"Kwin Airlines, Flight 474 will be taking off now!" announces the head flight attendant. "Fasten your seat belts and sit tight. Have a nice flight!"

Soon enough, the plane leaves the runway and takes its rightful place in the air. Flight 474 is okay and smoothly sailing the airstream. The passengers are relaxed. Maryann shoots a killer-smile at a male passenger who calls her attention in the "First Class" section; she had wished to be in this section and not the "Economy" section, and her wish came true.

"Sir, how may I help you?" she asks, politely.

"Oh, sorry." the passenger apologises. "I had a need, I don't have it anymore. I am very sorry. I will call you later. You are beautiful."

"Thank you, sir." Maryann replies, stepping away from the man in a professional way.

"You are welcome." the passenger replies with a smile.

Maryann returns to her standing position. She looks at the watch on her wrist and keeps her head erect immediately. Her clear vision reveals a young woman coughing, sneezing and bleeding through the nose. She goes to attend to her.

"Miss, you don't look good. What is the problem?"

"I'll be fine. Get me water, I need to take my drugs."

"Okay, be gentle on yourself. I'll be back in a jiffy." Maryann leaves to get a bottle of water. She returns immediately, and the young woman quickly grabs the bottle of water.

"What's the medical condition?" Maryann asks her fellow flight attendant (a nurse) who has just come to see the young woman.

"Don't worry, leave her to me. She will be fine."

Maryann leaves them; she walks away briskly. Her attention is on other passengers now. Minutes pass. Within few minutes of returning to her position, she sees a blue signal. She looks and sees a man beckoning to her. It is the man who called her attention before. He, probably, has a need now. She goes to meet him.

"How may I help you, sir?"

"Your name."

"What, sir?"

"Your name. What is your name?"

"Sir, please, I don't think I should be having this kind of conversation with passengers. My name is Maryann. How may I help you, sir?"

"Don't worry, I am fine. Thank you."

In a professional way, and without losing the smile on her face, Maryann walks back to her standing position.

Fortunately, she will need not to offload a great deal of distress and stress when the plane lands; this should be true due to the immense dwindling of the circumference of passengers' help-needing.

In just the right amount of time, the plane finds its rightful place on the runway of the Australian airport, Canberra Airport. As the passengers climb down the stairs of the airplane, Maryann and her fellow flight attendants try to ensure the safety of the passengers and that the plane is in good shape. Maryann's mind flits to the peppersoup she will have after the passengers leave the plane. She welcomes the thought with a relish.

A man, the same man who is full of needs he seems unwilling or a little willing to reveal, calls Maryann by her name. Maryann turns sharply.

"I am in Australia for a book fair. I would have been the happiest attendant if you were accompanying me. Truth from my heart." He beats his chest.

Maryann, smiling: "Oh, gee, thanks for the compliment. But why?"

"I will tell you why if you will spend some time with me at the airport café, but I doubt you will. Here's my card, call me. Make sure you do. Put down your phone number on this pad, you know the road to hell is paved with good intentions. I don't want to have a heart attack from waiting for your call."

Maryann collects the pad and writes her phone number quickly.

"Thank you, Maryann. Have a nice day."

"You too. Have a memorable book fair." She turns briskly and resumes the work of ensuring that everything is fine on the plane.

And so, that was it! One person called the other and one thing led to another, and a made-in-heaven relationship started. This is how Maryann found herself dating an Oxbridge graduate, this is how Maryann found herself dating a celebrated writer.

Soon, they are travelling together for major literary events - from book launch to book fair to literary festivals. Kelly Onwuka, whose real name is Kelechi Onwuka, will do anything to make Maryann happy. He often seems not to care about the considerable gulf in educational background, and so love often seemed to bridge the gap. At a book festival in Iceland, he tells Maryann a wonderful story of how his father broke down in tears when he saw his first book in his favourite bookshop. He was a writer-in-residence at an American university at this time. His father had been going to this bookshop after the Nigerian Civil War to teach himself general knowledge and to immerse himself in good literature. After a while he stopped going, but was overwhelmed on the day he returned to see Kelly Onwuka on a book spine. First, it was the surname that attracted him. So he picked the book and looked at the author's picture at the back of the book. Lo and behold, it was his son's picture! He broke down in tears because his son had never told him that he dropped medicine he sent him to study to pick up Comparative Literature. His father bought the book and returned home with a mixture of excitement and anger. He later called his son and things were settled amicably. On hearing this story, Maryann wipes the tears in her eyes and says, "What an emotional story!"

Now, let's pause here and ponder over a few things:

Does it mean Mr. Seth has no interest in beautiful Maryann?

Does it mean Kelly Onwuka has never fallen in love before?
Did Maryann ever meet Mr. Seth's brother?
Is Maryann truly in love with Kelly Onwuka?
Will this made-in-heaven relationship last?

Okay, let's go back to the story. Love is a beautiful thing, especially if the persons in love are faithful to each other. And no one should quickly conclude that a person is unfaithful until things have been verified and analyzed.

Anyways, on a vacation in Cyprus, Maryann walks into their room and finds Kelly Onwuka sitting on the bed with a beautiful chocolate-complexioned woman. They are going through notes and looking into a laptop. This infuriates Maryann and she goes to confront Kelly Onwuka. This will not be the first time she is confronting him. This is not the first time she is seeing Kelly Onwuka with women. On the first confrontation, Kelly Onwuka told her that women are his muses. He said that seeing them laugh, toss their hair or crack jokes inspires him. Of course, Maryann did not swallow his defense hook, line and sinker! Women are jealous beings and must be treated with caution. So, of course, Maryann enters and Kelly Onwuka sees her.

"Oh, goodness gracious!" he exclaims, stepping down from the bed. "Lady, meet the love of my life!" He is still gesturing towards Maryann. He sees Maryann raise something and a bottle of beer finds his *occiput*.

For heaven's sake, Maryann shouldn't have flung the bottle.

∗∗∗

She flung a bottle, a bottle full of beer. Let's fast-forward to post-flight attendant days. Well, you already know the story. Yes, you are right, Maryann is in jail!

CHAPTER SIXTEEN

THE ORCHESTRA OF FROGS

Year: 2024, Location: Jandun Forest.

"Frog legs, anyone?!" Meredith shouted.

The other children who were already farther ahead turned. The sky that have been overcast for long began to weep slightly. It was drizzling. The tall trees that had been shading them from the sun seemed otiose as they could feel the raindrops landing on their heads and clothes. It was six days since they have been marooned in this forest. Hungry and without food, they turned to things they wouldn't even dare near if they weren't lost. Anything could be meal. Frogs, birds, rats, anything that could make a tasty or crispy food. They were salivating for these foods like Adam and Eve for Eden's forbidden fruit. Meredith was the one who often kept the meal bag which she often carried on her back. It was a unanimous decision. She had announced that their roasted snacks was finished before calling out to them. Surprised, the hungry children began to run back. They were marooned because their school excursion helicopter heading to an archipelago had a pancake landing. And the pilot died the following day by being caught by an animal trap when he went to urinate upon a spruce.

"But you said the meat had finished." It was Kate's voice. The children had surrounded Meredith now. "Didn't you?"

"I did. But look, there's still plenty meat left."

The other children began to grumble and mumble.

"Don't play with people's life. How could you lie through your teeth?" said Wole.

"I am sorry for the joke that I was carrying wood for fire instead. Okay, let's line up." Meredith was the oldest, the more reason the other children felt she should be in charge of the bag of meat. The children had already lined up when Meredith produced a roasted frog leg from the bag. "This is for you." she said and handed the meat to Peter who was first in the line. Peter also known as Blue Jay didn't look too happy.

"Meredith, could you please add another leg to this!" Don't give me food as though I'm an ant."

"You are not. But the food isn't enough." Meredith said politely.

"Add some more, sister. A brother is sick with ravaging hunger."

"Step aside, Blue Jay. Let others have theirs." Adaeze said and pushed him away. His meat almost fell from his mouth. He complained and left the line.

"Greedy boy." Aisha said from behind Adaeze. "Always wanting some more."

Peter turned to her and scowled.

"Here's yours, Wole. Here's yours, Kate. Here's yours, Akwaeke..." A sudden violent movement that shook trees in the distance took words out of Meredith's mouth and left others shaking with fright.

The children clustered at a spot, packed like sardines, and watched carefully. The trees and grasses were still shaking, so the children were still shaking with fright. Still shaking when a wild boar appeared from the thicket. Still shaking when they saw the boar and its piglets.

"It's a wild pig." said Wole. "It's just a pig!"

"What do we do?" Adaeze asked.

"What do you think we ought to do? Of course, ignore it." Hilda said.

"Did you say ignore it? A little milk to spice up our diet will do no harm." Fred said.

"What?! *Nono banza! - nonsense milk!*" Aisha said.

"How do you even intend to milk the thing? Kill it first or just go to it?" Peter asked.

"Nice question." Meredith said.

"Go to it." Fred replied with a smile.

"Ha ha." Hilda laughed. "You are a joker. That thing will just mangle you. Don't mess with it, unless you have been yearning for some harm. I was even thinking in the line of making a meat out of it, but we don't have the weapon that can kill it without us being harmed in the process."

"Alright, people, let's have a detour. We will still get to the hunting ground by the longest route, only that we will waste time that could have been saved." said Meredith.

"God knows, I am tired of all this. I just want to go home!" Kate said. "I miss my family."

"Nobody wished to be here." Meredith said. "We are only here by circumstance and must act like a big family until we are rescued. I will keep sending out radio signals hoping that we will be rescued soonest. We will all make it out of here alive. Let's keep faith alive."

"Aye, captain!" Peter said. "Now, let's head to the hunting ground. Those animals have been waiting for us to grab them."

Everyone turned to the new route and the journey to the hunting ground began.

***

"Be careful. Look out for animal traps!" Meredith warned.

"Let's hope we meet any of these hunters. They will definitely be of help." Hilda said.

"Nice! Nice!!" exclaimed Wole. "None of us even thought of that, even though I presume they will be primitive. But I think they can still be of immense help."

"I totally concur." Kate said, throwing a dead rat into their bag.

Still drizzling, the weather became sunny again. Hilda looked up and said aloud: "It's a monkey's wedding. Don't this shade of leaves look like the Sistine Chapel?"

"Sistine Chapel my foot!" Peter said and threw a frog into their bag. "Is it by painting or what?"

Hilda, ignoring his rude first sentence: "I mean the leafy ceiling over us is so beautiful with the illumination from the sun. Isn't it beautiful?"

"Don't mind Peter, it's quite a beautiful sight to behold." Akwaeke said. "Too bad I left my camera at our locally-made tent."

"Please," started Meredith. "We must return early so that we can repair our broken tent. Plus we need to roast all of this before dusk. Peter, you must keep the lighters and matchboxes safe. We can't afford to lose them or have them spoilt. Alright, family, it's time to go home."

They ensured all their dead preys were inside their bag. They set about to go home.

***

Before sunset, the children had repaired their broken tent and ensured that their meats were properly roasted. The meat comprised of sixty percent frogs which were easier to get than rats and birds. It was not that the children wholeheartedly opted to make a meal out of frogs at the first suggestion from Kate. They had argued and refused. But Kate said she had a Chinese neighbour whose number one meat was frog. And that she had enjoyed it on several occasions. So since someone who had tasted the meat was in their midst, they gave in. They gave in and started enjoying frog meat. Taste buds accustomed, hunger a constant. Deprivation not an option, the children kept enjoying their frog meat. Sometimes they even preferred to eat their frog meat last. They could do anything for the love of frog meat. Anything. And so, like they usually do before it became dark, they gathered in front of their tent and sang and prayed. When they were done praying, they told riddles and jokes and laughed. Though on some occasions they remembered their predicament and cried afterwards. But overall, they were stronger for children their ages. Who amongst them knew they would land in someplace not an archipelago, in someplace filled with burgeoning disillusionment? Anyways, they were very hopeful. They had great belief that they would soon return to their respective families. Soon, night came and they built fire in front of their tent and sat by the fire eating and talking and laughing. And just like they have been doing, by seven-thirty p.m they would never be found outside their tent. Strong children, plucky children.

***

It was the morning of their ninth day in the forest, in someplace, not an archipelago. Half of them were already greatly frustrated, especially Akwaeke. As the morning chorus of birds rose, the children came out of their tent and built a fire. All of them sat down except Meredith who stood and observed the countenance of the others. Most were looking pensive. Meredith shook her head and sat down afterwards. She began to tell them things she felt would console them and uplift their spirits:

I observed how sad most of us are. I know we have reasons to be. It is understandable. But I do not want us to let frustration to get the better part of us. We must be strong. We must remain strong. I am still sending out signals. Today we all shall enter into the abandoned helicopter. We are going to pray in there. We are going to pray that God will hear the yearnings of our heart and save us, at most a day after tomorrow. We can't continue like this. This was not what we bargained for. This is not the archipelago we set out to visit. This place is not for us and we must leave it. I want us all to have faith. I want us all to be strong. We shall pray to see the light at the end of the tunnel. Now let's pray.

The children closed their eyes and prayed.

***

Afternoon of the ninth day. The children had finished having lunch. The girls were playing hopscotch, while the boys found a heavy wood and were tossing the caber. Wole said he felt he could tell where there is a river in a forest as they tossed the caber. Believe it, the children had gone without water for seven days! The only liquid that served as water for them was the coconut milk they got from harvesting coconut fruits from the coconut trees they discovered earlier on. The boys did the harvesting. But now, the fruits were no more as a result of popular demand. Now they must find another source of water, unless they could eat their meats without water. So when Wole announced to his fellow boys that he could discover water, everyone of them paid attention.

"So where can we find the universal solvent?" Peter asked.

"I think if we go this way we will find a stream." Wole said, pointing.

"Are you sure about this?" Fred asked.

"Maybe. Last night I heard running water sounds. I just might be right. Do we go now?"

"Sure!" Peter and Fred answered at once.

"Then let's inform the girls." Wole said and carried the heavy wood on his shoulder.

"Where are you taking that to?" Peter asked.

"To the tent. We still need it, don't we?"

"Sure, we still need it." Fred said. "I have proved I am the strongest and I want to do it again."

"Mr. Muscle. Your head is swelling with pride, right?" Wole said and walked on.

"Let it swell, man. I deserve it."

"Alright. Enough of your bragging." Wole said.

"Girls, girls!" Wole shouted and dropped the heavy wood in front of the tent. "I think I know where we can find water."

"What?!" they shouted.

"Water where?!" Meredith asked, hurrying towards the boys.

"I'm not sure where. But I know the direction we must move towards."

"Then let's start going right away." Kate said.

"Yes, we shall go right away." Wole said and carried the heavy wood inside the tent, with obvious aplomb, and closed the door.

"Let's go."

Excitedly, they hearkened unto Wole's command and followed his lead.

***

Deep into the heart of the forest they eventually went, blazing a trail that could lead them back to their tent. They walked on with Wole telling them that they had come too far to go back. And so, tiredly they walked on until Adaeze fell into a...a stream! And with a gasp of excitement, the other children rushed into the stream drinking and shouting. Girls were shouting Wole's name and praising him. The boys were shouting, *Water at last! Water at last!!* And it was not long before they started grabbing frogs by the stream. Fat, healthy frogs! Sumptuous-looking things. They were grabbing them by the dozen.

"So how do we take some water to our tent?" Hilda asked.

The children looked at themselves.

"Well, I have an idea." Wole said.

"Let's hear it." Meredith said.

"When we return we shall go to the helicopter. There is a metal container inside it, I don't know what it is for. We will use it to save some water. But, actually, the distance to this stream is not much; we can always return here before thirst becomes a killing thing."

"Okay. Settled." Akwaeke said. "Let's stay here a little longer. I mean I have been dying to have a bath."

The children sighed and agreed with Akwaeke. The boys left and allowed the girls to bathe first. They agreed to go away, but Meredith suggested that she go with them to ensure they didn't hide to peek at their naked bodies. She also suggested that a boy do like her too. The remaining boy and girl would take theirs with the boys and girls protecting them respectively. It was settled. So the children were able to have their first bath since being marooned in this forest. When they returned to their tent, they brought out their frogs and roasted them before going to fetch some drinking water.

***

When they returned from the stream, where they wasted time talking and trying to see if they could find fishes, they were exhausted and sleepy. But before they went into their ventilated tent to sleep, most of them tasted their newly roasted meat. They went in and lay their tired bodies down. And that was how they slept off, how they didn't hear when a rescue jet came hovering above their tent. It was already evening and the rescue team were eager to take them away before it was night. The men went into the tent and tried to wake the children. Only Hilda was able to wake. They gave the waking thing more trials but the remaining eight children did not wake.

"What happened to them?" one of the men asked.

"I don't know. We just ate and went to sleep. I mean they."

"What did they eat?"

"Meat. Frog meat."

"Goodness!" another man said.

"Maybe they ate a poisonous species." his colleague added.

"Oh, no!" Hilda cried.

"And why didn't you eat with them?"

"I wasn't feeling hungry, but my own share of the first tasting was given to me. Here it is."

The men shook their heads and began to carry the unawakened children to their jet. Hilda went in afterwards and the pilot drove off.

***

TNN Interviewer: "Okay, viewers! I know you all must have been dying for this. Here in the studio with me is Hilda Achebe, the only survivor amongst the children who were marooned in Jandun Forest. Welcome to the studio, Hilda."

Hilda: "Thank you."

TNN Interviewer: "So how did you feel when you realised you had escaped death?"

Hilda: "Confused. Just confused."

TNN Interviewer: "Can you describe the species of frog that led to the tragedy?"

Hilda: "Yes. They had fine colours. I found out they are called poison dart frogs. Their toxicity is said to come from the plant poisons which are carried by their preys such as ants, termites and beetles. Some nonpoisonous frogs have evolved to have similar colouring of the poisonous frogs to avoid being eaten by predators."

TNN Interviewer: "Gosh!"

Hilda: "I guess we were just too carried away by our growing love for frog meat to think about the possibility of having a poisonous species for food."

TNN Interviewer: "How did you guys turn to frogs as food? Whose idea was it?"

Hilda: "Well, it was Kate's idea. She said she had a Chinese neighbour whose best meat was frogs and that she had enjoyed it on most occasions."

TNN Interviewer: "Yes, before I forget. What happened to the helicopter taking you all to the archipelago?"

Hilda: "The pilot complained of some technical problems associated with engine and some other things, so he landed the helicopter in the forest and tried to repair it."

TNN Interviewer: "Quite sad. How did he die?"

Hilda: "He was caught by an animal trap."

TNN Interviewer: "That's really sad to hear. You are making a documentary whose title will be *The Orchestra of Frogs: A Brief History of Dying*. Can you say a thing or two about the project?"

Hilda: "Sure. The documentary is about how we danced to the tasty tune of the frogs and how my friends died by it. Everyone was expecting everyone else to get home to loved ones and friends. It's a tribute to my friends, my late friends."

TNN Interviewer: "Today is December 18. What are your plans for Christmas?"

Hilda: "I plan to join The Merciful Carol Singers. I will also give to charity."

TNN Interviewer: "So before we wrap up the programme, what do you have to tell viewers?"

Hilda: "Death was slightly hiding in plain sight. I am just lucky to be alive."

CHAPTER SEVENTEEN:

THE WEEKEND

From our houses on Banana Street, we go out to harvest and to thresh our dreams. We go out prepared. We, with our baskets, sickles, secateurs, winnowing forks and all. We are on our way to Freda Lake so we can catch the sight of The Rebuss. We all are going - Ugo, Uzo, Ada, Amy and I. It is Saturday and we are glad it is. Every kid who listens to radio, reads books or watches television has heard of Freda Lake and The Rebuss. Every kid from our block wishes to visit Freda Lake, and luckily for us we were able to save enough money. Ugo and I will take care of the boat fee, while the others will take care of feeding and other miscellaneous expenses. I know father would not have allowed me, but the heat of adventure in my bones says I must. I am sorry that I have to go where I must, and I hope to return with my heart desires met. We are on our way. Our driver is a cheerful man, and he is tickling Amy who is close to him. I hate to be tickled, but I am not Amy. We have to pass Lulu Road, and I hate it because the fish dealers pollute the air with their smoking. I often pass through Lulu Road because my father has a shop along this road, and we must pass the fish dealers to get to his shop. I make ready my handkerchief and wait. Uzo nudges me to show me the madman dancing, and we laugh together. Ada has just brought out her comic book, and Uzo and I are struggling to watch.

"You are stepping on me," Ada says in her usual saucy manner.

"Sorry," I apologise, with my eyes still fixed on the comic book.

"You are obstructing my view. Can you remove your head?"

I frown and jerk my head backwards. Uzo is begging her to open it wider, and I think Uzo is a fool.

"Let her watch alone, I have something to show you."

Uzo relaxes back, and I begin to open my schoolbag. Uzo's big eyes bulge like an ostrich's from a skewed lens. I open it wide for him to have a peek and he becomes excited immediately.

"Wow, big and plenty!" Uzo exclaims on seeing the apples. I turn to observe the countenance of Ada, and it seems to read:

Whatever that's in there must be good;
But of what use is it
When the owner will retaliate?

I smile as she takes a quick and focused look at me. I want her to beg me, not because I am willing to share my apples with her. I want her to beg me because I like her. Who doesn't know that Ada is beautiful? Yet, I have never had enough courage to wear my heart on my sleeves. I continue to observe her until she closes the book and Uzo begins to pester me for a taste of the apples. I quickly remove Uzo's hungry hands from my legs and sit with tight-face and hands tightly securing the important schoolbag. We are in a traffic congestion and, just now, Ugo feels like talking.

"Chidi, did you come with your catapult?" he asks from the front where he is sitting next to Amy.

I wonder what is with Ugo and catapults. We are going to see the three tail-finned Rebuss, and not flock of birds. I still answer him. "No. Thought I won't be needing it."

He is saying something else, but I don't want to hear it. We have just entered Lulu Road, and I must use my handkerchief or just die. I put the piece of cloth to my nose and wait for the smell of smoked fish and the soon-to-happen sudden reaction of my fellow travellers.

Just close to the centre of the block of fish shops, Uzo begins to scream.

"Oh gosh, what's this smell?! Please where is this rotten fish smell coming from?!" He raises the collar of his shirt to his nostrils.

I am shaking with knowing mirth.

"What is this smell?" Amy ask in her mellifluous voice. She looks out through the window. "Oh, these fish dealers shouldn't be selling by the roadside! This smell is very unpleasant."

I continue to laugh as the driver tries to speed away from the smell.

"Phew, what a relief!" Uzo exclaims.

"Yes, a real relief." I say before the driver remembers to say his mind.

"The local government of this area should remove those fish dealers from the roadside. How can one be inhaling such bad breathe in the name of driving through! This can't happen in..."

The driver stops talking as the sound of a burst tyre momentarily impairs our hearing.

"Ah, I believe I asked Adamu to change the tyres." the driver says and drives towards the hard shoulder in sight.

He stops the bus and waves at a mechanic standing at the other side of the road. "Please, I need your help!"

The mechanic, a haggard-looking thin man begins to approach our bus from the other side of the road. His blue overalls has a highly-visible oil and paint stains. As he stands to talk with the driver, his bald head comes to my notice. He looks thirty.

"Oga, wetin be the problem?" he asks.

"The problem is the tyre. *You fit change am for me?"*

"I no get tyre, but I fit get am from my guy shop. I dey come." He disappears to get a new tyre from his friend's shop. We wait for his return.

"Oh gosh, I hope this mechanic wouldn't delay our journey!" Amy says. The driver turns to look at her.

"Changing of the tyre won't take time, unless he doesn't return on time." the driver replies. "Don't worry, we will get to Freda Lake on time." I begin to assume the driver is an educated man due to his good English.

The mechanic hurries back with a new tyre.

"I hope that tyre is good." our driver says.

"Oga, this tyre no get equal. Na ogbonge tyre be this!"

"Fine, just fix it. We need to leave as soon as possible."

"Okay, oga." He squats to remove the damaged tyre.

Ada suddenly begins to laugh. I turn around and, lo and behold, Uzo is laughing with her - he has finally joined them to watch the comic pictures. I shake my head. I hold my jaw in my hands and begin to think about The Rebuss: 'how many tonnes can it possibly weigh? Can we possibly get a picture of its head?' I remember the argument and bet I had with Chisom: he said I could never save enough money to visit Freda Lake - *trust me, I paid him no mind. I eventually laughed at him.* I suddenly snap out of my musing as the driver starts the bus and we hit the road eventually.

***

Throughout the journey, my mind wandered from one thought to another. I imagined how beautiful Freda Lake, in reality, would look - I don't trust the media. Our bus keeps entering potholes, and I consider it a miracle that nobody has sustained an injury yet. At a police checkpoint, the driver kindly buys us snacks from the road hawkers thronging up and down the busy road. The policemen are still arguing with the driver, but now they won't anymore because the driver is holding out a hundred naira note. The oldest collects the bribe and we start speeding to Freda Lake.

From a distance, we can see a signboard that reads, "Freda Lake Ahead. 15 km. Slow Down, There's No Need To Rush." Despite the notice, which I think every one of us understands, the driver is still speeding to Freda Lake. Maybe, he wants to make up for the time wasted trying to change the damaged tyre. I dust my bag and stand instead - there is no need sitting when we will soon get down. I stretch my legs and my waist. Amy is chattering excitedly. Uzo stands suddenly, leaving Ada with her comic book. He puts his hand across my shoulder and we talk about The Rebuss and Freda Lake.

***

At the big blue gate leading into the land housing the lake, some tourist guides order our driver to stop. They peep into our bus, talk with our driver and then ask us to be of good behaviour and pay attention to instructions. We nod our heads and our driver begins to drive in.

As we find our way through the numerous shady trees, we begin to hear the voices of excited children. I am floating in balloon of immeasurable happiness; I wish to leave Freda Lake still floating, I wish nothing would deflate this my newfound experience. How I wish I am there already! Slowly, our bus parks at the parking space. I rush for the door, I push Ada aside and slide the door backwards. I jump down before everyone.

While others are coming down, I bring out my jotter and begin to read the things I jotted about The Rebuss:

"The Rebuss is a big, wide-mouthed fish with three tail fins. It has a spiky projection close to its three tail fins and can fly in the air for some seconds. The Rebuss was spotted in Freda Lake on October 7, 2071. Since then, this specie of fish has not been found elsewhere."

I close my book in time to join my friends and the tourist guide leading them to the lake. I am floating in balloon of happiness. I am full of beans.

The tourist guide takes us past a caravan with the inscription, "The Magician's House of Spells", before he decides to tell us what the caravan is all about. We return back.

"Briefly, this is where the lake's magician stays." he says, revealing his golden tooth to us. "Anyone who wants to see the magician must go with the guide standing over there." He points. "And the maximum number of people that can enter at a time is ten. Now let's proceed to Freda Lake."

His last sentence leaves me with a burning curiosity. Ugo taps my shoulder and begins to dance with a smile on his face. I shake my head, I have no time for such boyish madness. I increase my pace so that I can be just behind the guide's back, just in front of everyone.

On our way to the lake, the guide quickly points to a hut tagged "Apiary", and tells us that that's where bees are reared. Amy shudders, and I smile. I imagine a swarm of bees chasing her and closing up on her - I imagine her screaming and crying for help. Finally, we arrive the lake. There are so many children, so many children on colourful clothes. Most of the girls are in swimsuits - or should I say bikinis? The boys are on shorts and the older ones are separated from the girls. Just a stone's throw from the lake stands a clown. He is juggling and blowing bubbles out of his mouth. As we get close to the clown, our guide gives us serious instructions and leaves us with the many kids enjoying themselves. We thank him and run to join the crowd of happy children. Some children are watching the clown with rapt attention.

"Hey, remove your shoes!" one boy says to me. "Unless you want to have your good shoes messed up."

"Thanks," I reply and begin to remove them. "What is your name?"

"Moses!"

"Moses?! What a unique name! Nice to meet you, Moses." I put the shoes in my bag.

"Thank you. Tell your friends to get ready immediately; the boats would soon come."

"Oh, is that so?" Uzo asks from my back, startling me. "Hey guys, hurry up with the dressing or whatever. The boats will soon be here!"

Amy, Ada and Ugo begins to hurry towards us.

"Are the boats going to take us to The Rebuss?" Ada asks.

"Yes, my dear!" Moses replies. "But, according to what I heard, it may take long for The Rebuss to appear. Sometimes up to an hour."

"That much?" Ugo asks.

"Yes, but don't worry." Moses says. "We may see it within a couple of minutes, I always carry good luck with me."

"Hm. I hope your good luck works today." I say to Moses.

"We will be lucky." Amy says. "Who's that boy wearing a mask?"

"Oh, that one? He calls himself Cat-man, he's terrific. No single word leaves his mouth without you laughing. His mother is British."

"I see. I was wondering if he's white or once lived abroad." Ada chips in.

"Yeah, they call his kind *mulatto.*" Moses informs.

"What's the meaning of that?" Ugo asks.

"It means someone with a mixed parentage, someone who has one white and one black parent." Moses explains.

"Wow!" Ada exclaims. "I have always wished I had an American father."

"Really?" I ask. "I suspect you like blonde hair, don't you?"

"What's blonde hair?" she asks.

"A blonde hair is hair that is light yellow in colour."

"Oh, sure, I do! I love such curly yellowish hair."

"I love my black hair." Amy says, looking at Ada as if rebuking her for wanting something nature has not gifted her. "I love my black skin too."

"*Eh hen!*" Moses begins, throwing away the stone he was holding. "There is a rumour going around. I heard it from Cat-man. The rumour is about a brown house that opens to an island with children, robots and animals- animals that hear. I am really fascinated by the whole story."

"Is the brown house on this land?" Amy asks, her eyes wide with wonder.

"Yes."

"Hm, a brown house that opens to an island?" I ask.

"Yes, my friend!" Moses says. "It's a lake island and so it is called eyot. There, there are different ways of being. You are either a child or an animal or an android or nothing."

"There are no adults?" Ada asks with great interest.

"Yes, my beautiful one!" Moses replies. "Just children. Cat-man showed me the house."

"What?! Are you serious? So the brown house is real?" Ugo asks, surprised and excited at once.

"Yes, I saw the brown house. But we did not enter, and so we could not verify the existence of the island."

"We should do the verification before leaving Freda Lake!" I blurt out.

"Fine, I will tell Cat-man!" Moses replies.

"Please, tell him. I want to see the island." Uzo says.

"We will like to see the island." Amy says. "I'd like to see the animals. I hope there are zebras and penguins..."

"Hey guys, you see that girl over there?" Moses says, pointing in the direction of a girl wearing a white scarf with black polka dots. "She's been to The Bahamas. Her name is Ndidi. Come let's meet her, she's fun being with."

We move to meet the beautiful girl wearing a polka dot scarf round her bouffant hairstyle. She sees us coming and begins to smile. I am thinking about her long black hair, I am thinking about her oval face, I am thinking about what her accent would sound like, I am thinking about The Bahamas. We reach her in time to find out she is trying to hide something in the sand. I want to be the first to ask her what she is hiding, but I don't know if anyone has the intent of making a move. I restrain my impulsiveness.

"Hey, Moses, you've made more friends?!" she says, wiping her hands on her pink swimsuit.

"Yes. Guys, meet Ndidi." Moses says, putting his hand forward in an act of gesticulation.

"What's your name?" Ndidi asks me, bringing her hand out for a handshake.

"My name is Chidi." I say, almost intimidated by her sheer beauty and boldness.

"It's nice meeting you, Chidi." Ndidi says and begins to approach Ada. I begin to rub my palms in expectation. I can't wait to see how saucy Ada will react.

"Hey there, what's your name?" she asks Ada who is chewing her peppermint gum.

"Guys, guys, the boats are coming!" Moses shouts. Other children join in.

I swallow my disappointment and run ahead of my friends. Moses is in front. The guides are stopping us from getting too close to the land-seeking tongues of the waters. One boat has arrived and is being anchored. One huge man is shouting and asking us to form a queue if we want to pay for the boat ride. We are beginning to form a queue in front of a coconut tree, the excited children are pushing each other down. Luckily, I push myself into a space in the front - all my friends are farther behind, except Moses. They don't need to worry since I will be paying for all of us. To my amazement, Ndidi is the number one in the queue. I shake my head and try to write down our names on a paper so the huge man will know the number of people paying at once. I put down their names immediately and wait for my turn. The afternoon sun is scorching hot, everybody is sweating. I still wait for my turn amidst the shouts and flippant noises.

***

Finally, we are aboard our various boats. The sun is not shining so hot anymore. Luckily, we all are on the same boat - I, Amy, Ada, Uzo, Ndidi, Ugo and Moses. We are moving to the exact spot where The Rebuss do appear. One man on the boat is with a bag of something which I suppose is bait for The Rebuss. A boy with facial tribal marks holds his camera aloft, as if he is trying to flaunt his beautiful device. If left to my devices, I will just tell him to put the thing inside his bag and stop blocking my view – after all, we haven't seen The Rebuss yet. I contain my irritation.

As we get close to the spot where there is a red flag buried beneath, the same man carrying the bag of something begins to tell us not to throw anything into the lake or try to put our hands out of the boat. He looks in my direction and says:

"Do not try to play pranks. This is not a playground."

I nod my head - not because I think he is talking to me personally, but because I think I should. My imagination briefly wanders to the story of the brown house, and my curiosity is kindled. I see myself victoriously fighting some flying androids.

"What about the apples?" Uzo asks me, taking me out of my sweet fantasy.

"The apples? They are still in my bag."

"You don't want to eat them?"

I hate it when people ask stupid questions on what is not their business. "Uzo, I'll eat them when I want to. Please, watch out for The Rebuss. You may miss it if your mind is on apples!"

Uzo laughs; I wonder what's funny.

Suddenly, the waters begin to shake. Large ripples begin to form.

"Maintain a firm position!" the man of bag shouts. "It is The Rebuss!"

The camera-boy strikes a ready pose with his camera in his face. I keep my eyes wide open. I believe I am about to document enough stories that will leave Chisom lame with envy. Everybody is anticipating. I am expecting a flying fish with three tail fins. Now, our boat is shaking seriously. We are shouting. Man of bag is telling us to keep calm, and I wonder how we can. Our boat is still shaking. Something is dividing the waters, I can see it. Something long and sharp. Like a flash of light in a dark night, something heavy leaps into the air with its shiny glory. The Rebuss!

"There, that's The Rebuss!" Man of bag shouts. "I have to pour in this to attract its attention and keep it leaping." He begins to pour the content of the bag into the waters.

Camera-boy's device is going click, click, click.

"Get pictures of it!" I say to him impulsively. He does not seem to hear me.

Man of bag has just stepped back when this thing leaps into the air again, this thing called The Rebuss. Everybody is excited, and we are shouting.

"That's The Rebuss! Boy, that's The Rebuss!" Moses says to me.

"Yes, Moses! The Rebuss!"

The shouts begin to increase as the children in other boats catch a glimpse of The Rebuss. We are now on the Lake of Noise. I can barely hear myself now. Some people have blocked my view and I am struggling to see the waters or The Rebuss. Somebody is awakening my recognition senses with his shouting. He is calling a name. He is not the only one calling the name now.

"Ada has fallen into the lake, help! Ada has fallen into the lake, help!!"

I drop my bag immediately and rush towards the source of the alarm. I push down two boys standing in my way. Moving past them, I see some people staring into the waters in which Ada is struggling for breath, their hands flailing in the air as they scream for help. I run to where they are standing, I look down. I can see Ada gulping down water forcefully. I am thinking this cannot be Ada, I am thinking about salvation. With a flash of thought, I jump into the lake.

"Hey, somebody help! Two people are inside the lake!" That's the only alarm I hear, and now I can't hear anything as I battle with the waters, as I try to save Ada. I am breathing hard and fast. I think I am drowning, I think I don't know what I am doing. I am praying in a world of darkness. I know I need help. Suddenly, when I have started praying that my soul be received by God, a hand lifts me out of the waters. I do not know if the hand lifted me out now, but I know a hand is pressing my stomach and rubbing my face. I open my eyes, I close them. I open them again. Tears begin to surge through my eyes down my cheeks. I am alive! I stand. Everybody is either thanking God or shaking their heads. I look down, and I see Ada lying with a big stomach. I know this is not pregnancy, I know. I know this is stomach of water. I watch as two men try to bring Ada back to consciousness. I begin to imagine what our parents would do should Ada die. I ask God to forbid the tragedy. I notice that I am on a different boat. We are on a rescue boat. I remember my bag, I remember the brown house, I remember my apples and I remember that my friends are on another boat. Sadness begins to grow in my heart. I know my balloon of happiness has been deflated. It is already evening. I kneel near Ada. My whole body hurts. The sun is gradually becoming a deep orange ball. I am praying for a miracle. I am wishing, somehow, that I did not come to Freda Lake.

Mmap Fiction and Drama Series

If you have enjoyed *The Twins,* consider these other fine books in **Mmap Fiction and Drama Series** from *Mwanaka Media and Publishing:*

The Water Cycle by Andrew Nyongesa
A Conversation..., *A Contact* by Tendai Rinos Mwanaka
A Dark Energy by Tendai Rinos Mwanaka
Keys in the River: New and Collected Stories by Tendai Rinos Mwanaka
How The Twins Grew Up/Makurire Akaita Mapatya by Milutin Djurickovic and Tendai Rinos Mwanaka
White Man Walking by John Eppel
The Big Noise and Other Noises by Christopher Kudyahakudadirwe
Tiny Human Protection Agency by Megan Landman
Ashes by Ken Weene and Umar O. Abdul
Notes From A Modern Chimurenga: Collected Struggle Stories by Tendai Rinos Mwanaka
Another Chance by Chinweike Ofodile
Pano Chalo/Frawn of the Great by Stephen Mpashi, translated by Austin Kaluba
Kumafulatsi by Wonder Guchu
The Policeman Also Dies and Other Plays by Solomon A. Awuzie
Fragmented Lives by Imali J Abala
In the Beyond by Talent Madhuku
Zororo Risina Zororo by Oscar Gwiriri
Sword of Vengeance by Olatubosun David
Finding A Way Home by Tendai Mwanaka
Your Epistle by Solomon A Awuzie

The Restless Run and Ruin of the Roaches and Rats by McLayode
The Reign of Terror by Ntando Gerald
Ibala Lyabwina Nama by Austin Kaluba
Daddy, Please Don't Kill Mama by Natisha Parsons
Pilate's Angels by Goodenough Mashego
Blue threads and other stories by Matthew Kunashe Chikono
The Sylvia Plath Effect by Shakemore Dirani

Soon to be released

https://facebook.com/MwanakaMediaAndPublishing/